GA GA SEAT EVENT

SECTION ROW/BOX

BOGTROT CONCERTS PRESENTS

# HEADLINER

BY

## SUSAN WHITE

FREDERICTON, NB

SAT MAY 19, DOORS AT 12PM

GENERAL ADMISSION

05

THE ACORN
CHARLOTT
201

# ACORNPRESS

P.O. Box 22024
Charlottetown, Prince Edward Island
C1A 9J2
acornpresscanada.com

Edited by Penelope Jackson
Copy Edited by Laurie Brinklow
Designed by Matt Reid
Printed in Canada by Friesens

Library and Archives Canada Cataloguing in Publication

White, Susan, 1956-, author
Headliner / Susan White.

Issued in print and electronic formats.
ISBN 978-1-77366-007-3 (softcover).--ISBN 978-1-77366-008-0 (HTML)

I. Title.

PS8645.H5467H43 2018          jC813'.6          C2018-901117-3
                                                C2018-901118-1

  Canada Council **Conseil des Arts** for the Arts **du Canada**

The publisher acknowledges the support of the Government of Canada through the Canada Book Fund of the Department of Canadian Heritage for our publishing activities. We also acknowledge the support of the Canada Council for the Arts for our publishing program.

To Meg

# CHAPTER 1

*Design your perfect home.*

Finally, I was starting my assignment for Mrs. Taylor's Family Dynamics class. All semester, I had listened to her droning on about everything from emotional intelligence to the telltale signs of domestic violence. An assignment asking you to fantasize about the perfect home should have been no big deal. Put a 50-inch TV in every room, add a hot tub and a state-of-the-art sound system, and you'd have the perfect home. But in my messed-up head, all I could come up with were stupid ideas that mirrored just how totally screwed up my family was.

A home appropriate for the Callaghan family would have consisted of only a few rooms. The kitchen sure wasn't getting used much. You could make a peanut butter sandwich anywhere, and you could eat takeout and throw away the containers in any room. Mom definitely needed her bedroom and the bathroom, since she was always either in bed or taking a bath. Dad and Jenny would just need a place to keep their suitcases—not that they were ever home long enough to unpack. My room would stay, but the room across the hall from mine wasn't necessary. Nobody had even gone in Mike's room in the ten months since he'd left on the bus trip with his orchestra.

A perfect home would have been the home we'd had ten months ago, but I didn't know it then. I was just the middle kid in a family that looked like everyone else's. Mrs. Taylor had started the semester with a chart on the SMART board showing all types of families. The family we had been was on the chart, but the family we were now was not. We were off the charts, so to speak.

How would someone describe the family we had become? A missing mother only seen occasionally, speaking to the family through the closed door of her bedroom or the en suite bathroom. Travelling father and younger sister, home long enough to wash their clothes and re-pack before heading to the next competition so sister could be an Olympic speed skater. Dead brother only seen in the photos on the wall and never spoken about since the day of his big funeral and all the news coverage of the tragic accident that killed eight members of the Ridgewood High School Orchestra and one teacher. Middle child going to school every day, afraid if she stopped she would become like the mother and never be seen again.

Barely able to see what I'd written on the paper in the dim light of the late afternoon, I turned on my desk lamp. Last year, Mom and I redid my bedroom and I'd picked out the deep pink swivel lamp for the top of my desk. It had been way past time to change up my room from the princess theme I had chosen when I was five. I went with bold stripes in different colours and the pink on the lamp matched the top stripe. Stripping the Ariel wallpaper was challenging, and Dad had to fill some cracks and dents in the wall. Mike and I put the first coat of primer on before carefully measuring and taping the wall so Mom could paint the stripes.

The bright light shone down on the piece of paper. *Well, at least someone's paying the power bill.* I crumpled it up, throwing it into the wastepaper basket. I'd start again after grabbing something to eat. I could give Mrs. Taylor the crap she was expecting. I could play the game. I played it every day when

I left the house and pretended the Callaghan family was doing just fine.

"Mom, I'm going to make a grilled cheese. Do you want me to make you one?"

"No."

"Did you eat anything today, Mom?"

I didn't hear her answer. When I'd come in from school there'd been no signs of cooking or any dirty dishes in the kitchen. Mom always used to rush in minutes before us from her job as an EA at the elementary school. Something was always cooking. I used to love trying to guess when I walked into the mudroom what it was I could smell. Mike was better at the nose challenge than me or Jenny.

"Fajitas. We're having fajitas. I can smell the onions."

"Chocolate chip cookies."

"She's making that stir fry I love. I can smell the ginger."

Mom always had supper started and always something baking for our lunches. We had the best bagged lunches, and Dad's leftover meals were the envy of his office.

Opening the fridge door, I picked up the milk carton, shaking it to see how much was left. The expiry date, which was six days ago, discouraged me from unscrewing the top. There were two cheese slices in the fridge and half a loaf of bread on the counter. I'd make two grilled cheese sandwiches and take one up to Mom. Surely by the time I finished the sandwiches she would be out of the tub.

My phone beeped just as I was flipping the second sandwich. Looking at the notification, I could see it was a text from Bethany.

Bethany Thompson and her mom had moved here in January, and Bethany hadn't made a lot of friends yet. Not any of my old friends, anyway. They'd quickly made it known that they didn't want to have anything to do with her. The circle of friends I'd had since kindergarten was not exactly open to new things or new people. But someone new was exactly who I was looking to hang out with.

In that circle, Tara had been my best friend, and she had been right there for the first little while after Mike died. She'd even slept over the night before the funeral and stayed right by my side for weeks afterwards. All that caring and compassion somehow turned into the hurtful words she had blurted out a couple of months before.

Bethany wanted me to come over. The first time I'd walked into her apartment, I knew Mom would never have approved of me hanging out there. It used to be embarrassing when Mom called parents and did a drive-by assessment before she let me go to a friend's house.

It wasn't Bethany's fault that her mom could not afford a nicer apartment in a nicer area. It would be snobbish of Mom to think just because someone lived on Macgregor Ave. they weren't fit for me to be friends with. She'd always let me have friends come here, but unless she knew the parents, she would not let me go to their houses. She definitely would not have been impressed with the drug dealing going on in the parking lot of Bethany's apartment building. But that wasn't Bethany's fault either.

"Will her mother be home?" was always Mom's first question. So what if Bethany's mother wasn't even home the night I stayed there? There'd been one of those chain locks across the door. Mom didn't even realize I'd stayed all night. I didn't stay the second time; the party started to get a little out of hand. When guys Mike's age started coming in, I got out of there. I didn't need to be reminded by a bunch of jerks that my brother wasn't there anymore. I walked all the way home that night, wishing beyond wishing that I could have called Mike to come get me.

Mike always played the part of big brother better than I even appreciated at the time. It made me so mad when he put the run to Ethan Rogers when he tried to date me in grade nine. I was thrilled when Ethan started paying attention to me. He was the best-looking guy in the school. Ethan was in grade twelve, and Mike didn't mince words when he told me why a grade twelve guy would want to date a grade nine girl. He'd been right on about Ethan. Now, two years later, Ethan Rogers had two kids with two different girls. Mike used to make me mad, but I always knew he'd look out for me.

As the party got louder that night, it was the music that really sent me out the door and on my long walk home. Don't Feed the Wolf. When Mike had started listening to that band, I thought they were awful. I was all about boy bands at the time, the predictable pop that Mike made fun of continually. "A musical intervention," he called it when he would give his pitch for the kind of music he loved.

I cut the two sandwiches and headed upstairs, taking the first bite of mine. We had never been allowed to eat in any room but the kitchen or, on special occasions, the dining room. Sometimes we were allowed to set up the TV tables and eat in front of a show on nights when Dad would bring home pizza or Chinese. Mom said it was uncivilized.

"We're not animals, Michael. We eat at the table."

"Actually, we are animals, Mom. Homo sapiens with erect posture, bipedal locomotion, and manual dexterity."

Mike would tease Mom about all kinds of things. She never seemed to get mad at him, though. He was the funniest, kindest, most generous kid I'd known. Everyone had liked Mike. *Easygoing, helpful, an old soul.* Those were some of the things people wrote on his Facebook page after he died. At first, I looked at it every day. I couldn't get enough of the good things people were writing. But after a while, and not just because nasty comments were sneaking in among the nice ones, I realized just how phony all the gushy messages were. Most of the people who wrote didn't even know Mike. Some of them were the same kids that had given him a hard time at school for being a cello player.

I'd stopped looking altogether when the teacher who failed

Mike twice in a row and kept him from graduating wrote a long comment about what a great kid Mike had been. The bastard. Did he not think for one minute that if he had passed Mike, he would not have been on that bus trip? He would have been at Mount Allison, already getting the music degree he'd dreamed about.

"Mom, I made you a sandwich."

She was still in the bathroom, so I set the sandwich on her bedside table.

"Okay, I'm just getting out of the tub."

Funny how just a feeble "okay" was enough to put my mind at rest. For now, she hadn't drowned herself in the tub or whittled away with her razor at the purple veins on her wrists. For now, she was okay; as okay as she was these days.

Bethany let me into the apartment. She quickly fastened the chain lock.

"I kind of ripped off Max Davis and he'll probably come looking for his money. I'm just going to leave the light off and maybe he'll think I'm not home. It's crappy that we can't go out, but we can hang out here for a while, anyway. I got you something."

Bethany passed me the Don't Feed the Wolf vinyl; I'd looked at it when we were in the mall last week.

"You bought it! I still don't have any money, but I'll pay you back as soon as I can."

"Don't worry. I didn't pay anything for it. Max gave me money to steal a bunch of vinyl and I didn't quite deliver. It's a pain in the ass trying to get them through that security beeper and they're too big to put under my shirt. Don't know why anybody even wants them, but I guess some kids collect the stupid things. I kept a couple for myself and this one for you. If he doesn't like it, he can do the stealing himself. He's too much of a coward. Wouldn't want his doctor daddy and his hoity-toity mother to find out he's a thief. He'd hang me out to dry fast enough, though, and God forbid he would invite me into his fancy Kennebecasis Park home. Do you want some ravioli? I just opened a can."

"No, thanks. I ate already. Aren't you afraid of getting caught?"

"Stealing is no problem if you do it right and move fast enough. You've got to psyche people out and not show any fear."

"Have you got your assignment done for Family Dynamics?"

"Yeah. I did that yesterday. I really laid it on. Indoor swimming pool, wine cellar, and a hot pool boy. What about you, you done?"

"No. I can't seem to get started."

"Why not? From what I've seen you've already pretty much got a dream home. Two-storey house on a nice street, two-car garage with a car in both sides. Bet your TV works, not like this shitbox. Mom got it off the curb. Nobody wants a TV the size of a compact car anymore. Why did she think they put it on the curb, for God's sake? Had to drag the thing home, though, like she was doing me some big favour. I'm saving up for a flat screen. She won't even notice, not likely. I'm not sure what the point is, though. We can't afford cable."

Bethany had never mentioned where her mother worked. Bethany was always well dressed, had the latest iPhone, and always had spending money, which seemed a contrast to the little bit of shabby furniture in the apartment and the bare walls. Bethany's shoplifting income probably explained the difference.

Mom was on an extended leave of absence from her job. Dad had gone back to work after the funeral but had been on leave since Christmas so that he could devote his time to Jenny. This time they were away for three weeks. Somewhere in Ontario. Dad called every couple of days but didn't say much.

Lots of money and my parents' time had gone into Mike's musical abilities. He had settled on the cello five years ago and they bought him his own instrument. They didn't get it back after the accident. Apparently, most of the instruments were destroyed when the bus flipped over. And Jenny was born skating, but in the last few months she'd been totally committed to speed skating. It couldn't be cheap to outfit her for that sport, let alone the travel costs and hotels. I thought Jenny had sponsors who were helping to pay for the expenses, but no one really told me anything. But poor, talentless Franny didn't require much financial support, energy, or time.

I walked across the room and spooned up a bowl of the little pockets filled with what looked like ashes, smothered in a sauce that looked more like blood than pasta sauce. One grilled cheese hadn't filled me up. Why not let Chef Boyardee feed me? No one else was bothering to these days.

"When we're done eating, I'll write your assignment for you," Bethany said. "Who do you know who can bullshit better than me?"

I'd only been home from Bethany's for a few minutes when the phone rang. I counted six rings, waiting for Mom to pick it up, but answered it on the seventh ring.

"You're still up, Franny? I suppose Mom is sleeping," Dad said. "Sorry I called so late. We just got to Oshawa this afternoon and Jenny had a practice tonight. She's in the shower. She's exhausted. She is working her butt off. Two days here, then we go to Kitchener for her competition. How are things there?"

I considered my answer. Did he want to hear that Mom was the same as when he left? Did he want to hear that I'd been at my new friend's house, a new friend that he didn't even know, and I'd smoked my first joint tonight? Did he want to know that the stunned way I felt afterwards was a whole lot better than my normal feeling? Did he want to know that the milk was curdling in the fridge and I only had five dollars, which wouldn't even buy my lunch at school tomorrow?

"Everything's fine," I answered. "Say 'hi' to Jenny for me. Mom's sleeping. I'll tell her you called."

"Love you, Franny Bear. I'll call earlier tomorrow night so I can talk to your mother."

"Love you, too, Dad."

I opened Mom's door a crack. When I called her name, she didn't roll over.

"Dad just called," I said. Lowering my voice to a whisper, I added, "I need you, but don't worry about it, Mom. I'll be fine."

Tears streamed down my cheeks. It pissed me off so much when the tears came. I was usually really good at keeping them away. No big deal if I let them come right now, though, when not another person in the house would hear me crying or care. I tore the cellophane from the album, took it from the sleeve, and set it on Mike's player.

Mike had been so proud when he bought his turntable at Staples. I'd teased him and said he could play his albums on the old Fisher-Price record player, or play music on his phone, like the rest of our generation.

"It's their new album, Mike," I said aloud, my voice rising above the music. "I don't think I can give it the critique that you could. I hear the bass, but I don't know shit about the rest of it. Broken chords, modulation, and cadenza: that was the language you used. I don't know anything except that I miss you."

# CHAPTER 2

Five dollars got me Hickory Sticks, a bottle of water, and a package of Skittles. All the major food groups covered. I was definitely going to have to convince Mom to go for groceries or to give me some money to at least get milk, bread, and a few things I could carry home. Mom had hardly driven lately, and getting her to leave the house had been next to impossible. Even getting her to get dressed and leave her room was a challenge. Dad didn't even bother to try when he was home and conveniently only called after she was asleep when he was away.

The first time he convinced her to go out in the early weeks did not go well. They'd just sat down at Mom's favourite Thai restaurant when Jane Finlay came in. Her son Thomas had been best friends with Mike since playschool. Thomas was sick with the flu the week of the orchestra competition and stayed home. If he'd gone, there was no doubt he would have been sitting with Mike, and he'd probably have been one of the kids killed or at least seriously injured. Sadie Daniels was paralyzed and would be for the rest of her life, the doctors figured.

Jane had walked right over to Mom and Dad's table. She could have, I suppose, just turned away when she spotted them. Some people did that, thinking we wouldn't notice.

To be fair, I did it quite often, too. I was getting really good at scoping out a place and making quick getaways. I did it just about every day at school. So far, I'd been successful in dodging any real conversation with Tara. Mrs. Finlay could have darted the other way, but she came right over.

Mom's retelling of the words Jane offered certainly sounded callous, hurtful, and insensitive. I'm sure she hadn't meant them to be.

"So good to see you out, Marilyn. I'm sure after all the fuss it feels good to get back to normal. I'm just picking up some pad Thai for Thomas. It's his favourite. You know how growing boys are. I just can't fill him up."

Mom and Dad didn't even order. Dad brought Mom right home and she took to her room for the rest of the night. The next day, she just kept repeating the words *fuss* and *normal* as if they were the two most offensive words in the English language. I understood where she was coming from, but part of me felt sorry for Mrs. Finlay, too. I'd stupidly put my foot in my own mouth more times than I cared to think about.

Going out was still a bit of a minefield. Three days before, I had seen Mrs. Reynolds, who used to babysit Mike when Mom first went to work. Apparently, she didn't listen to the radio, watch the news, or get the paper; or maybe at her age things just got fuzzy. Whatever the case, she stood behind me at Tim Horton's and asked how my family was. She asked me how old Mike and Jenny were now. I stood there awkwardly.

The girl behind the counter had asked me for my order. I waited for Mrs. Reynolds to get her coffee, then sat at a table with her. I was hoping she would realize her mistake, but even when she started talking about the years she'd babysat Mike and what a darling boy he'd been, I wasn't exactly sure whether or not she knew that he was dead.

"I just hope I live long enough to see you kids have children of your own. That Mike is so talented. What a handsome boy, too. Does he have a girlfriend yet?"

"Mike died." I'd said the words slowly, almost in a whisper. I'd wanted to just get up and run out of the coffee shop. I hadn't wanted to hurt the dear old lady. I didn't mean to embarrass her or make her uncomfortable. But I couldn't sit there and listen to her talk about my big brother as if he were still around, as if all the things she was hoping for him were still possible.

Maybe I should have worn a sign. In bold letters, a sign could announce that my brother Mike was dead. Maybe the sign could give a few simple instructions, like "Don't be afraid to say his name" or "A quick 'I'm sorry' is fine." The sign could even say, "You can still talk about your own life and we will understand." Really, the sign would have to be way too big. Maybe just a sign that said "Death Sucks," or "We are doing the best we can," or "Don't be afraid of us." No simple sign would do it, because it was not simple. Not at all.

Mrs. Reynolds had taken my hand. Tears streamed down her cheeks. "I am so sorry. Your poor mother."

I felt like I'd ruined her day. She could have gone about her business without knowing that the little boy she babysat seventeen years ago was dead. I hated that my presence always brought that truth along with it. Maybe that was the main reason I found hanging out with Bethany easier than spending time with my old friends. She didn't even know Mike, so she didn't have to think about him every time she saw me, search for the right words, or say anything about him at all.

"Mom. We need some groceries," I said, loud enough that she turned over and faced me.

"What?"

"We don't have anything in the house to eat, Mom."

"Is your father home?"

"No, Mom. He and Jenny are in Ontario. They won't be home until Sunday night. I can just walk to the store and get bread and milk if you don't feel like going to the grocery store."

"Give me a few minutes and I'll get ready to go. Make a list of what you think we need."

I walked downstairs and sat at the kitchen table. I ripped a piece of paper from the back of my Chemistry notebook and started a grocery list. I jotted down the basic stuff first and then started to think of what would get us through the next few days. I didn't cook much. I'd never had to, as Mom always had a handle on the meals, sometimes planning for a full week ahead. Our cupboards and the fridge used to always be overflowing.

"Shotgun." The request was redundant, of course, but came out before I could stop it. The fight for shotgun once all three of us were big enough for the front seat had gotten so bad at one point that Mom had come up with a system to end the arguing by assigning each of us a week on the calendar.

Mom gave no indication she'd even noticed my unnecessary request as she slid into the driver's side. She backed out of the garage and I turned my head to hide my tear-filled eyes.

It was only a short drive to the Superstore, but I watched each block pass by in slow motion. I honestly couldn't remember the last time I'd been in the car with Mom.

"What day is it, Franny?"

Her question jolted back me to reality and I wasn't sure I'd heard it correctly.

"Sorry, what, Mom?"

"What day is it?"

"It's Thursday."

"What's the date?"

"March 20. You know what year it is, right?"

"Well, yes, I know what year it is."

I wanted so badly to reach over and touch Mom's arm, but I may as well have been in the minivan sitting beside us at the red light.

Mom pulled into a space in the Superstore parking lot but didn't reach to unfasten her seatbelt. "I really don't feel like going in. There should be money in the account. Do you think you could take my bank card and get the groceries? Did you make a list?"

"Yeah. Anything you feel like having?"

"No, not really. Get whatever you want."

"What have you been eating, Mom?"

"I don't know."

I didn't know what to say to that. I was well aware of the bareness of the cupboards and could not imagine what she'd eaten in the previous couple of days. She'd definitely lost weight in the last ten months. When she'd stood before me a few minutes earlier in jeans and a blouse instead of her daily costume of baggy pajamas or a bulky housecoat, it hit me just how thin she was. It was a tough weight-loss plan to just take to your bed and stop eating.

At first there had been almost too much food. People kept arriving at the door with dishes. Tupperware containers filled the countertops and casserole dishes filled the refrigerator. Aunt Lesley put a lot of it in the freezer. By the time she went back home, the steady stream of sympathy food had dried up and we lived off the freezer food for a few weeks.

"Okay, Mom. I'll go pick up some stuff. I won't be long."

I quickly filled the bottom of the cart in the frozen food section. Mom used to walk right by this aisle and seldom gave in to our pleading. Mike had gone through a Pogo phase, but Dad was the one who fed that. We all had a fondness for fish sticks and fries, though, and even Mom would allow that once in a while. It was actually a comfort food that somehow ended up being prepared strangely. Dad liked his in the normal way, but the rest of us ate what came to be known as "smushed-up."

Mom had invented it when she was a teenager. Dad's guess was that some type of substance abuse was responsible for Mom first taking the pastry blender and mashing the French fries and fish sticks together, then mixing enough ketchup in to make a soupy mess. She denied that but could never really say what made her smush them up in the first place. "It's just like a fishcake," was her explanation.

Whatever the origin, we all loved the bowls of smushed-up Mom would dish up for us while Dad ate what he considered a civilized plate of intact fish sticks and French fries. It was an interesting dish, considering Mom's usual standards when it came to cooking.

I threw a bottle of ketchup in the cart just in case we didn't have enough at home to do smushed-up right. I would make some for Mom and me when we got home. I set three loaves of bread in the cart. I added some canned soup and a couple of cans of tuna.

I headed to the produce department and picked up a bag of oranges, a bag of apples, and some bananas. As I dropped a bag of salad mix into the cart, Mrs. Drummond, Mike's grade four teacher, came up behind me and wrapped her arms around me.

"Franny Callaghan. God love you, dear. Just getting a few groceries? God love you, dear."

The weird interaction was over before I had a chance to even respond. I quickly darted to the dairy aisle. I recognized two people, but they turned their carts away quickly. I picked up some cheese, a tub of yogurt, a two-litre carton of white milk and one litre of chocolate, and then I headed for the checkout. At least with fresh milk, Mom could eat cereal when she didn't feel like getting anything else ready.

I entered Mom's PIN and waited for "Approved" to show up on the screen. I would have been so embarrassed if the debit card was denied—but it went through. I lifted the bags into the cart and took the receipt from the cashier, then looked at her name tag. I thought she looked familiar, but it wasn't until I read her name that I realized she was the girl Mike took to his grade nine dance. Melanie. He'd been quite smitten with her. She hardly even looked up at me and I wasn't sure if that was just her normal customer service skills or if she didn't want to make eye contact and admit she knew who I was and feel compelled to say something to me about Mike.

"Thank you, Melanie," I said as I lifted the last grocery bag.

She did not respond, but loudly and with more enthusiasm than necessary asked the woman behind me for her PC Plus card. Lately I did not share Mom's aversion to going out. I made a game of it. I kept a tally in my head.

People seemed to fall into one of three categories.

There were the *gushers*, the ones who hugged, teared up, or went to great lengths to say how sorry they were, how terrible it was that Mike had died, and how devastated they were.

There were the *avoiders*, who usually ducked out of sight and did anything they could to not have to talk to you.

The last category, the *ignorers*, in my opinion hurt the most. They talked to you, but acted as if nothing had happened at all. The ignorers talked about the stupidest, most trivial things and never mentioned anything related to Mike or the accident.

I would sometimes quickly evaluate the possibility of the ignorer really not knowing. As they stood there complaining about the weather or something, I would try to remember if they'd been at the funeral parlour or the church, or if they'd stopped by with food or sent a card. There were people like Mrs. Reynolds who genuinely had no idea, but in a small town like Quispamsis, they were few and far between. Once I'd established that they knew what my family was dealing with, I resisted the urge to go into a rant putting their petty concerns into perspective for them and usually just ended up walking away from their tedious small talk.

As I headed to the car, I tallied the grocery store interactions. Mrs. Drummond was a gusher; two avoiders had dodged me in the dairy aisle; but Melanie hadn't run away. Even though she hadn't actually spoken to me other than to state the amount of my grocery order and ask whether I was paying with cash or debit, I counted her as an ignorer.

Avoiders had it hands down on this outing. That was the way it usually played out. Maybe if I had told Mom my findings, that the odds were she wouldn't have had to talk to anyone, she would have felt more like going places.

I picked up Mom's bowl from her bedside table. She'd eaten some of her smushed-up, but at least half was still in the bowl. She was sound asleep, so I turned off her light. She had been crying when I got to the car with the groceries. I tried to get her to talk to me, but she just kept saying she was sorry. After pulling into the garage, she'd hurried into the house. By the time I took up her supper, she was in her pajamas and back in bed.

We never had regular conversations. I rarely told her anything about school or what was happening with me. She said sorry a lot, and every time I opened my mouth, my first urge was to say sorry as well.

*Sorry Mike is dead.* That went without saying. We were all sorry about that. *Sorry I'm alive.* Dumb, but how I felt sometimes. *Sorry no one is really talking about anything or making an attempt to figure out the best way to be a family again.* We used to play our parts, but those parts had changed when one of the leading cast members died.

I did the few dishes in the sink and finished putting the groceries away. Bethany had texted me several times since school but I hadn't returned her texts. She wanted me to go over, but I really didn't feel like hanging out there that night. I wanted so badly for Mom to give me the out I knew she would have if things had been normal.

Bethany had offered me a joint on break that afternoon, but I had no intention of being that kid. It was bad enough that I was now hanging out every break with the smokers who rushed out to the road between classes, lighting cigarettes and standing around like idiots. I wasn't going to start smoking cigarettes, either.

Mom and Dad had made the deal with us that if we didn't start smoking by the time we were eighteen they would pay us two hundred dollars. Mike got his money on his birthday, five weeks before he died. He negotiated a fifty-dollar maintenance payment to be paid every birthday until we turned twenty after convincing Mom and Dad that the added incentive was necessary to help us resist peer pressure at university.

Mike would not get his two maintenance payments, but I planned on making his negotiations worthwhile. Besides, I couldn't afford cigarettes. And for sure I did not want to get caught at school with pot, which would just add to Mom's troubles.

And then there was the shoplifting. It was common knowledge that Bethany could get pretty much whatever you were looking for and sell it to you at a discounted price. Most days her backpack was full of crap in the morning and by the end of lunchtime she had sold everything. She seldom bothered to put a textbook in her backpack. Coming to school for Bethany was a business enterprise—definitely not a learning one. People had already started asking me if I was selling stuff, too.

Mom had always told us, "You are known by the company you keep."

My phone beeped and I looked down at the incoming text. *I'm coming over.*

What harm could that be? It would be better to hang out here anyway.

*Sure. Mom's sleeping; we'll have to be quiet. A movie?*

"Nice house," Bethany said as she walked through each room as if she were on a tour with a real estate agent. "My whole apartment would fit in this room."

Something about the way Bethany was picking up things and looking at every detail in the family room was making me uncomfortable. Funny how you didn't even notice stuff until you looked at it through someone else's eyes. I felt protective of everything in the room. Stuff that others wouldn't think was important told the story of my life. The old quilt that we always used to cover up with was folded on the arm of the couch. We used to fight over that spot and the quilt when the three of us were watching something together. Mike always seemed to get the good spot and Old Betsy. He'd named the ragged quilt Old Betsy a few years ago. We were lucky if he let us share the couch when he'd settle in and lay full out across the three cushions.

I picked up the folded quilt and quickly stuck it in the closet. I didn't want Bethany to make fun of it or casually wrap up in it. I looked at the framed pictures that covered one wall: all our school pictures from kindergarten up. I was hoping Bethany would not feel the need to comment on any of our ridiculous outfits or any of my hairstyles. Jenny had always kept her hair long and usually pulled back in a ponytail, but I'd been more adventurous. And Mike had gone through a hat stage from grade seven to grade ten. In grade ten he wore the cowboy hat he had bought on a trip out west with our grandfather. He looked like a young country singer nervously auditioning for *The Voice*.

"Nice cowboy hat. Your brother Mike, right? Max told me you had a brother. Bus accident?"

I picked up the remote and clicked on a pay-per-view channel. "Want to order this one?"

"Sure. I don't care. Be all right if I stayed the night?"

"I guess. Business deal gone wrong again?"

"Mom's bringing a guy home and I don't stick around if I can help it. They don't come to meet me. How come your mom's in bed already? Is she sick?"

"She's just not doing so great."

"Where did you say your dad and sister are?"

"They're in Ontario. My sister speed skates and Dad takes her all over the place for competitions."

"Cool. Must be great to have this big house all to yourself most of the time."

I picked up the phone to call for the movie. Having the house to myself wasn't such a great thing and I was kind of glad to have Bethany's company. I'd almost called Tara a few nights before when being alone seemed unbearable. She used to sleep over at least once a week, often Thursday. Mom had always been more lenient toward the end of the week, and Thursdays seemed almost like the weekend. The previous year Mike had been allowed to take Mom's car on Fridays because he had orchestra after school, so we got to sleep in and get a drive with him in the morning.

Mornings had been hectic and evenings always a chaotic dance of mealtime, homework, activities, and Mom and Dad's meetings. The comings and goings required Mom's careful planning and organizing, but on Thursdays we were all at home. Thursday was often takeout and family time and watching *How to Get Away With Murder*. Thursdays were now the hardest night of all to be alone.

All of our activities had come to a screeching halt in May. Mom gave up the two volunteer groups she'd helped with. She gave up choir and stopped going to her knitting group. Dad stopped playing hockey on Wednesdays and stopped being a Cub Scouts leader. He'd started volunteering with the Cubs when Mike started, and had stayed with it. He loved it, and I know it was hard for him to give it up, especially when camp time came. The only thing he kept doing was taking Jenny to the rink three early mornings a week—and now the travelling. They got caught up in the frenzy of a new routine and Mom and I stayed behind to do nothing.

"I suppose you don't want me to smoke in here."

My first instinct of course was to tell her no. Mom never let anyone smoke in the house, not even Dad's brother, who smoked in his own house and thought talk about the danger of secondhand smoke was a conspiracy against smokers. He and Mom got in heated debates, but Mom always stood fast on the rule and even in the coldest weather insisted he go outside. My next quick thought was that if I let Bethany light up, Mom would smell the smoke and come out to see what was going on. She would have to acknowledge Bethany's presence and might even show some curiosity over the fact I had a new friend, a smoking friend.

"Yeah, go ahead. I'm going to get some chips and get ready to watch the movie. It starts in ten minutes."

# CHAPTER 3

As soon as the last bell rang, I went quickly to the grade nine wing, hoping Mr. Riley would have Jenny's work ready to give me so I wouldn't miss the bus. Once a week whenever Jenny was away, I picked up her schoolwork. She did it when she came home and I returned it. It amazed me that she kept up and made better marks than I ever thought of getting, even though she wasn't in school regularly.

I, on the other hand, had technically been here every day, and I was barely passing two of my courses and definitely flunking the other three. The thing was, I was there in body only. My mind and my attention were somewhere else. Right after Mike had died, all the teachers seemed really sympathetic and understanding. They didn't even make me write my final exams. First semester this year, there still was a bit of leniency from all my teachers, except Mr. Johnston, who basically wouldn't let up on a kid unless the kid herself died. I'd passed his class first term partly because I'd always loved history and partly because I was scared of Mr. Johnston.

Scared in a good way, though. Mr. Johnston had been Mike's favourite teacher, too. Mike had always struggled in school. He was talented in so many areas, but not reading and writing. Mr. Johnston always gave Mike his tests orally and he aced them. Too bad he hadn't been that successful in grade eleven Math. For two years in a row, a few marks off passing kept him from graduating. He never showed just how much that bothered him.

"More time to get better on the cello," was his reasoning. "And more time to save for university."

"How is Jenny making out?" Mr. Riley said as he passed me Jenny's work. "Pretty exciting that she's so close to qualifying for the Commonwealth Games. Tell her I can give her an extension on the book report due next week. She's probably not getting much time to read. Mrs. Mackenzie sent three Math quizzes. She said your mom or dad can just sign them and she'll assume they supervised her and didn't let her cheat."

My bus was just pulling out onto the main road as I ran out the front door. Chatty Mr. Riley had explained every assignment and asked way too many questions. After what seemed like an endless Jenny-fest, his last question had thrown me for a loop. "How are you doing, Franny?" It seemed like a harmless enough question, but it was the way he said it.

"You can't let yourself get lost in all this," he said. I'd rushed from his room, from his hand on my shoulder and from the look in his eyes. The walk home wouldn't kill me.

I hoisted my backpack onto my shoulder, now weighted down with all Jenny's books as well as my own, and started walking across the parking lot. Max Davis pulled up beside me in his parents' SUV and lowered the window. I could see Bethany, Marin Donavan, and Sam Allaby sitting in the back seat, not trying to conceal the joint they were passing back and forth even though several teachers were walking to their cars.

"Want a drive?" Max asked.

"Is she even big enough to ride in the front seat?" Sam called from the back.

I was small for my age. Lots of times people assumed Jenny was older than me. I had only just started developing and was self-conscious about my lack of breasts, which I usually hid beneath layers of clothing. Sam Allaby had been my nemesis since middle school. We were never really friends, and she'd made a sport of picking on me when we started grade six. She was definitely not my favourite person.

And getting in a vehicle with a teenage driver other than Mike would mean breaking one of my parents' strictest rules. "Teenage brains and driving don't mix," Dad always said. When I started high school, that was the rule Mom repeated the most. "You can always call us. Never get a drive with anyone, no matter the circumstances."

She hadn't said it lately—hadn't really said much of anything lately—and she was proving that first part untrue these days. Even if I called her cell phone, she was unlikely to answer it. Why would I bother walking home just to avoid breaking a rule she didn't seem to care about anymore?

I opened the passenger door and jumped into the Pathfinder. I squeezed my backpack down at my feet. "Are you going by Oakwood Acres?"

"We're headed to Marin's," Bethany answered. "Her parents won't be home until late and Max has a case of beer. Come with us. He can drop you off later."

Great. Not only was I breaking the rule about not driving with a teen driver, it was likely that later I'd be driving with someone who'd been drinking. Max was probably already stoned, though, so what the hell.

"Sure, why not. I don't have any other plans."

It was after ten when Max dropped me off at the end of my street. Walking along the sidewalk, I looked in at the lighted rooms on the familiar street. I knew most of the families, and I lingered in front of the houses of the people I knew best. The Dixons were the first couple we'd gotten to know when we moved into our house. Eleven years before, Ron and Alice were just a bit older than Mom and Dad were now. Their youngest daughter, Laura, had been our babysitter until she went to university. Now she lived in Alberta and had two kids of her own.

Laura had cried so hard at the funeral parlour. She was so upset. She hugged me for so long. She'd flown home for Mike's funeral. That had meant a lot to Mom. Ron was sitting in his recliner by the large picture window, snoozing maybe. Alice was walking toward the window to close the curtains, probably aware that someone was on the street staring in.

If I rang their doorbell, I knew they would be more than willing to welcome me in. I knew, too, that if I told Alice just how difficult a time Mom was having, she would go out of her way to stop in more, to try to encourage Mom to go out or to maybe get some help. But I didn't want Alice to smell liquor on my breath. Ringing their doorbell and letting them know how messed up everything was didn't seem like an option.

I kept walking and looked into the basement window of the next house, where I could see Mrs. McEachern sitting at a quilt frame, stitching away. Mom had taken a quilt-making course from her a few years before and made a baby quilt for Aunt Lesley when she had Jordan. I looked at the colourful quilt Mrs. McEachern was working on and thought about knocking on the window. It would scare the life out of her, but once she saw it was me, she would ask me in. Maybe she could help Mom.

The next house was in darkness, just as I figured it would be. I stood looking at the darkened windows, wishing so badly that Mom had at least left the front light on for me. Had she even noticed when I didn't come home after school? Was she lying awake worrying about me? Had she called any of my old friends looking for me?

I sat on the curb and let the tears fall. I should have choked back a third bottle of beer. If I had, maybe I would be feeling better. I pulled my arms inside my jacket, shutting out the chill of the March air. I could hear a dog barking and saw the lights of a car on the street over. I stood up and walked around to the back door.

Lying in my bed, I thought about the evening I'd just spent. For the most part, I'd been uncomfortable the entire time and wished I had just walked home. When we first got to Marin's, she and Max went right upstairs to her bedroom. Sam was busy on her phone and Bethany was clearly focused on casing the Donavans' house, helping herself to a bottle of wine she found on the kitchen counter. I sat nervously at the kitchen table, trying to block out the sounds from up above.

When Marin came down, she ordered a pizza and I felt like a dork with no money to offer her toward it.

"My treat, anyway," Max said. "It's been a good week, thanks to our light-fingered friend here." He offered a toast to Bethany and took a big swig of his beer. I, on the other hand, took a minuscule amount and swished it around in my mouth, trying not to spit it out. I hated the taste. Sam emptied the wine from the first bottle and Marin opened another one.

We moved into the family room and sat around awkwardly, Max flicking the remote nonstop until the pizza delivery guy showed up. While Marin went to the door, the light-fingered Bethany picked up a small silver box from the coffee table and slipped it into her backpack.

Sam only said a few insulting things all evening. She seemed to like it better when there was a big crowd around, like in the cafeteria a couple of months before when she made an insulting remark about some kid in orchestra and then quickly followed it up with a backhanded apology to me. She hadn't exactly said, "All cello players are fags except the dead ones," but that's what it sounded like to me.

Bethany had called a few other people, but no one else showed up. I managed to drink two cans of beer, one disgusting sip at a time, and the long evening finally came to an end. Even though Max drank the rest of the case, I was happy to get in his vehicle and get out of there.

The drive home was uneventful. I took a seat in the back, making sure Sam got shotgun, and except for slamming on his brakes when I told him where to let me out, Max did okay driving. Bethany tried to convince me to come to her place to sleep over, but I figured I'd had enough fun for one night.

I looked in on Mom. Nothing. No sign that she'd even missed me. I checked the answering machine before heading upstairs and listened to a message from Dad. They would be home late Sunday night. Great, I had the whole weekend to get through. But after tonight, I was happy to spend it alone in the comfort of my own home. I would start by sleeping in as long as I wanted to in the morning.

I tossed and turned a while before getting back up and putting Don't Feed the Wolf on Mike's turntable. I kept the volume low, listening to the first five songs. The sixth one was my favourite, and I replayed it a few times before lifting the arm and turning off the player. It probably would have been Mike's least favourite, though I had nothing to base that on except the fact that I liked it. We had never seemed to agree on music.

We had the same taste in other stuff for the most part. I'd always got him Christmas presents he liked. It had been so hard this year getting through the season. Mike always made Christmas morning an event. He'd make a big production of opening his gifts, especially from me, even though I gave him a Grateful Dead T-shirt for five years in a row. You would have thought I'd designed it myself, the way he went on about how cool it was every time.

This year it had been awful. I didn't even care that Mom barely did any shopping and there was hardly anything under the tree. Even the absence of the tasty traditions Mom always spoiled us with was not the worst thing. The hardest part was Christmas Eve, when there had been no ornaments to open. That was always the last thing we did before going to bed. We'd put our Christmas pajamas on, have a cup of hot chocolate, set out Santa's milk and cookies and a carrot for the reindeer, and then open our ornaments.

Mom had always picked an ornament that seemed to match exactly what we cared about that year. I'm not sure how Hallmark knew what the Callaghan kids were up to, but Mom always found just the right one every year. We would open them and ceremoniously hang them in the spot on the tree with our ornaments from previous years, signifying where we would locate ourselves in the morning to open our gifts. It was a big deal. A big, drawn-out, important deal—but Mom hadn't done it this year.

She hadn't even wanted to put a tree up, but Dad overruled that decision. Jenny and I decorated it, even taking Mike's ornaments out and hanging each one. Leaving them in their boxes was not an option we even considered. I'd undecorated it a couple of weeks into January. Dad and Jenny had left for two weeks of training in Halifax, and it looked like no one else was going to bother taking the tree down.

I had boxed up all Mike's ornaments but left them on the top of the bookshelf in the family room. They were still there. I'd stopped noticing them until Bethany picked one up the previous night then took the time to look at each one. I had left the room, not wanting to hear or respond to any of her comments. The next day I would put them away with the other Christmas things in the closet under the stairs.

# CHAPTER 4

It was after twelve when I woke up. I showered quickly and headed to the kitchen, feeling dehydrated and hungry. Mom was pouring a cup of tea. She barely acknowledged my entrance.

"Hi, Mom. Looks like a nice day."

"Yeah."

Mom used to say we were sleeping our lives away when we would sleep past noon. "Half the day is gone," was one of her favourite lines. "This isn't a hotel. Breakfast is only served once," was another one. After we had made ourselves something to eat, she would give out the Saturday chores, which would tie up our afternoons. And Saturday night suppers often included some of our favourites: baked beans and brown bread, Mom's famous mac and cheese, or lasagna. It seemed like a lifetime ago since I'd tasted any of Mom's cooking. Saturday suppers always made Saturday chores bearable.

I slathered some peanut butter on my toast and poured myself a glass of milk. "Dad and Jenny will be home tomorrow night. We should make lasagna or something so they have food when they get home," I said.

"If they are going to be late, they will have eaten before they get home. I'm sure they're not missing any meals."

"We could eat it and then they can have leftovers on Monday," I continued.

"I don't know if I have any of the ingredients."

"Tell me what we need and I'll look. If we need something, I'll walk to Sobeys and get it later. Do you want me to vacuum?"

"I don't care. I'm going back to lie down. Maybe tomorrow I'll feel like making lasagna."

"I can make it if you tell me how."

"We'll see." Mom picked up her cup of tea and left the room.

"We'll see," always used to mean yes. The three of us had used a strategy when there was something we wanted. Sometimes Mom would give a definite *no* to the first one to ask. The next one might get a maybe, and then we'd send Mike in. If he didn't get a yes right away, she would give him a "We'll see."

"She said we'll see," Mike would come back and state triumphantly. Usually a short time later the answer would be yes.

"You are putty in that boy's hands," Aunt Lesley used to say to Mom. "Mothers and their sons," she would add, "and fathers and their little girls." Mike certainly had a way of getting Mom to come around. Jenny definitely had Dad wrapped around her little finger. Where did that leave me?

After finishing my toast, I walked into the family room. Before I vacuumed and dusted this room, I would put Mike's Christmas ornaments away. With a bit of cleaning and cooking, I would make Dad and Jenny think everything was just fine while they had been away. Maybe if I could convince them that Mom was getting better, I could convince myself, too.

Mike had had eighteen Christmases. His Baby's First Christmas ornament was there. The ornament he got his second Christmas broke the year the tree fell down on Boxing Day. Mom tried to glue it together but ended up throwing it away. When Jenny was two, she snapped the hockey stick off the hockey player ornament that said *Son*, but Mom didn't throw it away. Every year when Mike hung it on the tree, he would say something about the hockey player with no stick. I didn't remember any other ornaments being broken, so there should have been seventeen ornaments all in their original boxes.

Dad said they would be worth money someday—just to bug Mom, I think. "They won't sell their ornaments, Doug. They are priceless. They are something they will always have from their childhood."

"I hope you're right, Marilyn. Hope there never comes a day when they sell their memories on eBay to pay their rent or buy their drugs."

Sixteen small boxes. I counted twice to make sure. I set the boxes in a row by year. 2005 was missing. I looked at each box carefully, trying to think which ornament 2005 was. Over the years there were snowmen, hockey players, beavers, and one that said "Like Father, Like Son" with a big and a small pair of boots. There was a mug of hot chocolate, a gingerbread house, a box of Crayola crayons, a moose with earphones listening to music, and a violin case, which Mom said was a cello case, of course.

What ornament was missing? I racked my brain to remember Mike hanging them up every year. Every year, Mom would take a picture of us holding our ornament beside the tree on Christmas Eve, so if I had to, I could go through the photo albums to figure out which one was missing. A boy holding his sister up to a mailbox. A boy dragging a Christmas tree behind him. A snow globe. Santa on a tractor, reindeer sitting around a bonfire.

The Lego one. That was the one missing. A Lego fireplace that Mike got the year he started his love of Lego that never went away. It was his favourite ornament. He always hung it first, commenting on the detail of it. His Lego ornament had been there when Bethany looked at them Thursday night. It was one of the ones she took out of its box to look at.

I counted the boxes lined up on the couch again. The Lego one was definitely not there. I looked at the top shelf of the bookcase and on the floor around it. I looked around the room, thinking that maybe Bethany set it somewhere else.

Last night, Bethany had stolen Mrs. Donavan's sterling

silver box.

I knew Bethany was a thief, but I didn't think she would steal from a friend's house. It didn't even matter how much the silver box was worth; it was the principle of the thing. Maybe that box meant a lot to Mrs. Donavan. Stealing from a friend somehow seemed worse than stealing from a store, even though I knew that was wrong, too.

Could Bethany have taken Mike's Lego ornament?

I took the vacuum cleaner out of the laundry room closet. I could not stop thinking about the possibility that Bethany had stolen Mike's Lego ornament. God knows what else she might have taken. I would keep my eyes open for anything else that might be missing. There wasn't anything valuable lying around. I'd taken every bit of change from the bowl on the hall table days ago.

The only liquor in the house was a bottle of cooking sherry Mom used for something. Mom had a little bit of jewellery, but nothing really expensive. I knew Bethany wasn't in Mom and Dad's room Thursday night anyway. Was there anything in my room worth stealing?

The Lego ornament wasn't really worth much, despite what Dad had said about selling them on eBay. But it was worth something to me. She'd stolen a part of my brother's history, and that meant more to me than money. She'd crossed the line. Enough was enough.

I turned on the vacuum cleaner and attacked the living room carpet with the rage I felt picturing Bethany helping herself to Mike's ornament, slipping it into her backpack the way she took Mrs. Donavan's silver box. I would text Bethany and casually ask her if she put it somewhere. Maybe there was an explanation.

*Did you put my brother's Lego ornament somewhere?*

I thought about the question before sending it. It gave her the opportunity to say if she put it anywhere besides her backpack. Maybe she set it somewhere else in the house—although why she would, I didn't know. Maybe she would say she put it in her backpack by mistake. Sounded stupid, and she would have no reason to do that, but if she offered some excuse for taking it I might overlook it.

I considered just coming right out and asking her if she'd stolen it. Maybe she would just apologize and that would be it. Getting it back was the main thing, although if she admitted to taking it our friendship would never be the same. It wasn't as if we were so close. I barely knew her and really what I did know about her wasn't making for a great friendship.

I kept waiting for a response. Usually she answered my texts right away. I set down my phone and took the vacuum into the front hall. I would finish vacuuming downstairs before I checked again.

*No*

That was all she wrote. What was I supposed to do with that? Her saying she put it back with the others or giving some attempt to explain why I couldn't find it would be better than just a stupid no. Should I follow it up with, "Did you steal it?"

No. I would save that confrontation for the next time I saw her. But how would I handle a denial or a confession? Either way, I wasn't looking forward to having to get to the bottom of it, or what I dreaded most: not being able to get to the bottom of it. I didn't think Bethany cared one way or the other just how much the ornament meant to me and how betrayed I felt that she would steal it. If I knew anything about Bethany, I knew she didn't care a whole lot about people's feelings, about honesty or answering to anyone else's idea of right and wrong.

Mom came out of her room for a while Saturday night. She even noticed that I'd vacuumed and thanked me. She sat in the family room and started watching *The Notebook* with me. Who didn't enjoy a sappy love story when they'd not gotten out of their pajamas for two days? Every time a commercial came on, I would try to start telling Mom about Friday night. I wanted so badly to blurt out just how stupid I'd been to go to Marin's when everything I felt pointed to it being a bad decision. I wanted to tell her how I had heard her voice in my ear all evening. I wanted to tell her how disappointed I was coming home to a dark house and the fact that she hadn't even noticed I wasn't home or how late I was getting in.

I wanted to cry and tell her how much I wanted my mother back. I wanted to feel her arms around me and see some emotion that belonged to *me*. As selfish as that sounded, I wanted some of her tears to be for me. I choked back my words and the tears that welled up when that thought crept in.

"Mom, you're not going to bed, are you? Ryan Gosling hasn't even come out the door in the pink blanket yet. That's always been your favourite part."

"I'm tired."

My grandmother Darrah always used to snap, "What have you done to be tired?" at us whenever we used tiredness as an excuse.

Somehow, though, I thought Mom would not find her mother's quote funny just now, so I didn't say it out loud. I didn't say any of what I was thinking out loud. Mom went to bed and I sat watching the rest of a movie with which I was so familiar I could have muted it and filled in the dialogue myself.

I was so anxious for Dad and Jenny to get home. I didn't even care if they talked nonstop about Jenny's training, finish times, and ice conditions. Just having someone else in the house would be a welcome change. At one point, I'd even second-guessed my refusal to invite Bethany to come over or go to her place. My rage had calmed, but my feelings of hurt and betrayal had not. Part of me wanted to get the confrontation over with, and another part wanted to completely forget about the whole thing. I settled somewhere in the middle and simply got through the weekend.

In the end, Mom's "We'll see" had not meant yes. She did not make or teach me to make lasagna. She did, however, tell me to cook some hamburger, and she actually cooked a pot of macaroni and opened a can of tomatoes on Sunday afternoon. A pot of macaroni was a long way from Mom's delicious pan of lasagna, but I was glad to sit down with a plate of it at suppertime on Sunday.

I hadn't seen Mom much all day, but around six-thirty she came downstairs, dressed and looking better than she had for a long time. She'd even used the curling iron on her hair and put on makeup.

"Mom, I've already eaten, but do you want me to heat up some macaroni for you?"

"No, that's all right. I'm just going to have tea and toast. Sorry I haven't been much company this weekend."

I didn't say anything. It had been a long, quiet weekend, but did she honestly think she'd only been poor company the previous two days? I got up from the table and put my dishes in the dishwasher. I would wait for Mom's plate and cup before putting it through. The dishwasher used to run at least once a day, but it now took more than a week to fill it up.

"I got Jenny's schoolwork from Mr. Riley on Friday, Mom. She has quite a bit of catching up to do."

"She'll get caught up with no problem, I'm sure. It amazes me how dedicated she is."

I knew that Mom's compliment to Jenny wasn't meant as an insult to me, but I took it that way. When she used to go on about how great Mike was on the cello, part of me always felt just how much of a failure I was on the piano, on the recorder in grade five, and on the violin the one year I took it at school. Mike was a natural musician, just like Jenny was a born skater and a perfect student. But what talents were hiding under the surface for me? Nothing had shown itself yet.

I laid out my books on the kitchen table. Maybe engaging or looking like I was engaging in schoolwork would prompt

Mom to ask me about school. I tucked my last three Math quizzes in the back of my binder. The red lines, the X's, and the pitiful mark on the top of each of them were not what I wanted to open that dialogue with. I opened my Chemistry textbook and began answering the questions on my assignment. It had been due Friday, but, if I was lucky, Mr. Henderson would accept it tomorrow. Possibly I still had some "Mike Callaghan's poor sister" leverage.

Dad and Jenny came through the door at nine forty-five. I rushed to them, and without restraint, I crumpled in Dad's arms. I didn't even try to hold back the tears streaming down my face. Jenny set down her suitcase and joined in the hug, wrapping her arms around me from behind. It seemed a long time before I let go and pulled myself out of the embrace.

"Glad you guys are home." I said the words quickly and clipped the ending, turning away from my own vulnerability.

I met Mom coming into the kitchen as I was walking out. I had had my reunion with Jenny and Dad and I would let her have hers. Maybe tomorrow we could get back to figuring out how to be a family again.

# CHAPTER 5

I saw Bethany standing at the corner of the school when Dad dropped Jenny and me off. Dad had made his signature French toast for breakfast, and we were running a bit late. The bell would ring soon, so I walked right into the school. I would talk to Bethany later.

Despite going to bed early, I had been a long time getting to sleep. I'd felt overwhelmed by the homecoming. I'd known I was resentful, but it wasn't until Jenny wrapped her arms around me that I knew just how angry I was. It took everything not to whip around and tell her to get her hands off me. But what good would it have done to take it out on her?

Staying in the kitchen and watching Mom go through her own masquerade of convincing Dad that all was well would have been way too much for me. At least if they were staying home for a month, some of the things that needed addressing might actually come out in a more natural and less explosive way than me having a hissy fit in the first few minutes they were home. Dad was going back to work, and Mom had gotten up and actually sat at the table with us when we ate our breakfast.

I could hear them when they had come upstairs the night before. Jenny was talking a mile a minute, telling Mom all about her tryouts. Dad peppered the conversation with praise and added details. I hadn't heard Mom say a word. The last thing I heard Dad say was something about Mom going back to work, but their bedroom door shut and I did not hear her response.

Maybe that was the answer. If Mom got back into a regular routine, maybe she would start acting like herself. *Acting*. Were we all acting? Dad acting like the doting father. Jenny acting like the capable, amazing fifteen-year-old with a world of possibility. What part was I acting? Whatever it was, I wasn't doing a very good job.

I wasn't paying the least bit of attention; my thoughts were on my next class, when I would be sitting beside Bethany and either saying something right away or ignoring the ornament discussion completely. I considered how the first approach might go:

"Did you put the Lego ornament back in the box?"

"Yeah."

"Did you put it back on the shelf with the others?"

"Yeah. What's the big deal about the ornament? I put it back, okay?"

"I can't find it anywhere."

"You think I stole your brother's stupid ornament? Is that why you blew me off all weekend?"

"Well, did you?"

I figured we'd both swear, and I'd be no farther ahead. My brother's "stupid ornament" would still be gone.

"Franny, do you have an answer for number seven?"

We were checking the assignment together. When I'd tried to pass it in to Mr. Henderson at the beginning of class, he said he was glad to see I'd done it but it was too late to get marks for it.

After offering my answer, which surprisingly was correct, I sank back into my preoccupation with confronting Bethany. No matter how I played it out in my head, it never ended with Bethany admitting and apologizing or in any way understanding how big a deal it was for me.

The bell finally rang, and I filed out the door, heading for my locker.

"Want to skip next class?" Bethany said, coming up behind me and scaring the crap out of me.

"No."

"Fine, be a pussy. Marin and I are heading to Tim's. She's got her mother's car."

"Did you steal my brother's ornament?"

"Screw you."

I walked into Mrs. Taylor's classroom just before she shut the door. The dreaded confrontation was over, faster than I'd imagined but just as final. No confession, no explanation, no tearful handing over of Mike's ornament. Pretty much what I expected, and the end of the friendship. No big loss, I suppose, but friends were something I didn't have an over-abundance of these days.

I slipped into my seat, trying hard to pull it together. It wasn't the confrontation or my disappointment in Bethany that was choking me up. It was the fact that one of Mike's favourite ornaments was gone, and someone I trusted not only took it but didn't care in the least how important it was to me. And maybe even more than all that was the hurtful realization that there was no one I could talk to about how I was feeling. My first go-to had always been Mom.

Doing a quick scan of the cafeteria, I did not see either Bethany or Marin. The trip to Tim's would not have taken all morning. Maybe Marin having the car was the opportunity Bethany needed to refill her inventory. The thought of Mike's orna-ment stuffed in with all the other things Bethany offered for sale made my blood boil. But it wasn't as if a 2005 Hallmark Christmas ornament was going to be a hot seller.

Sam motioned for me to come sit with her. I looked toward the table by the vending machines, where Tara and my former friends always sat. I went and sat across from Sam.

"You didn't go with Marin and Bethany?" Sam said. "I had a Math quiz."

"No. I didn't think they would be gone all day, though, did you?"

I wasn't sure why I was letting on that I cared one way or another if Bethany was gone for the day, for a week, or forever. I picked up my sandwich and took a bite.

"No, I just thought they were going for coffee. I'm not all that keen driving with Marin anyway. How she got her license, I'm not sure. She can't drive for shit."

"How was your test?"

"Okay, I guess. You're not in my class, are you?"

"No, I've got Mrs. White for Math. My brother had Mr. Donaldson."

I didn't continue.

"I'm going out for a smoke," Sam said. "You coming?"

"No. I'm going to the library. See you later."

Bethany did not show up for last class and I didn't see any sign of her at bus time. I was happy the day was over. It wasn't until the bus pulled onto my street that I realized Jenny wasn't on it. She must have stayed after for something. Might have been nice of her to tell me that, although it wasn't as if I was used to her being around anyway.

As soon as I walked into the mudroom, I smelled food cooking. I stood a minute trying to determine exactly what I was smelling. Coming up blank, I walked into the kitchen to find out.

"I've got a roast beef in the oven," Mom said.

I looked around the kitchen and could see that Mom had been busy. A rack of cookies was cooling on the counter and the sink was filled with vegetable peelings. Several pots were on top of the stove. The table was set. I felt just about ready to burst with emotion. Except for one place missing at the kitchen table, it was just like old times. I didn't know what to say.

"I'll go upstairs and do my homework before supper, Mom." I wanted to hug her and tell her how wonderful it was to see her, how great it was that she was in the kitchen. I wanted to acknowledge what a big deal it was, but I chose instead to pretend it was no big deal at all.

If I acted like coming home to Mom dressed and supper cooking was nothing out of the ordinary, maybe we could just ease back into something similar to before. I took the steps two at a time, genuinely anxious to get my homework done and have the rest of the evening unfold in the regular uneventful and comfortable way evenings used to happen here.

Once in my room, I put the Don't Feed the Wolf record on the turntable. I set the arm carefully onto the middle of the album. The song was fast and rhythmic. I picked up my huge stuffed gorilla. A few years before, Mike had won the ridiculous looking stuffed animal at the Gagetown Fair and had given it to me. It was so ugly it was cute. Months before, I had dressed George of the Jungle in one of Mike's Grateful Dead T-shirts. I hugged George close and danced around my room with him.

"I miss you, Mike. I miss you more than ever, but Mom might be back. I need her back, Mike. I need her back."

I fell onto my bed and buried my face in Mike's shirt, letting the stuffed gorilla muffle any sounds of my crying.

I was finished my English questions and was almost done my Chemistry assignment when I heard Mom's voice downstairs. Dad or Jenny must be home. I closed my textbook and headed down to the kitchen.

Mom was sitting at the kitchen table crying. Only two plates were on the table now. I sat down beside her.

"What's wrong, Mom?"

"Your father just called. He and Jenny won't be home for supper. He said he told me this morning that he was picking her up after school for practice, but I don't remember him telling me that. I was so looking forward to sitting down and having supper together."

I put my arm around Mom. "Oh, Mom. Did he know you made a big supper? What time will they be back? We can just wait and eat when they get home."

"No, there's no point. He said they won't be home until after ten."

Mom stood up and picked up her plate and cutlery. "I don't feel like eating. You go ahead before everything gets cold. I'm going up to bed."

I took my plate to the stove and got some mashed potatoes, carrots, and a spoonful of corn. I took a piece of roast beef from the plate on the counter and spooned gravy onto everything. Mom had even made gravy. I sat down at the table and took the first bite despite the lump in my throat and the anger I felt.

I picked up my phone.

I typed *Are you home?* and hit send.

Seconds later, Bethany answered with a happy face emoji.

I texted back. *I'm coming over.*

I finished eating my supper and put my dishes in the dishwasher. I thought about putting the vegetables, meat, and gravy in containers and putting them in the fridge. But I wanted Dad to see the meal Mom had prepared. He probably wouldn't even realize what an important breakthrough it was. All the time and energy Mom had mustered to make a supper, for nothing. Dad probably had no idea what a slap in the face he and Jenny not showing up was for his wife, and just how disappointing the ruined family supper had been for his daughter. His other daughter.

I went to the mudroom and grabbed my jacket. Maybe coming home to the dried-out food would wake him up to what was going on in this house. If that didn't do it, maybe his daughter not coming home all night would.

# CHAPTER 6

Jenny squeezed into the bus seat beside me at the end of the day.

"Dad and I overslept this morning. How come you didn't wake us before you left for the bus?"

I stared at my sister, quickly taking in what she'd just said. They thought I had taken the bus that morning. No one even realized I hadn't come home the night before. No one in my family bothered to open my door to say hello or good night. What a change from the bedtime routine we used to have.

We used to have a regular routine that Mom called "Good night, John-Boy." Apparently when Mom was a kid there was a show called *The Waltons* at the end of which, every night, the whole family would go through the exercise of saying good night to each other. The oldest of the large family was John-Boy. We'd always finished with "Good night, John-Boy" after we took turns saying "Good night, Mike," "Good night, Franny," "Good night, Jenny," "Good night, Mom," and "Good night, Dad." "Good night, John-Boy."

I'd hated every minute of being at Bethany's the previous night, but I made myself stay, with the hope of having Dad call my cell phone and, after finding out where I was, rushing right over and reading me the riot act about leaving without telling anyone where I was and for going somewhere without permission. I had looked forward to Dad descending on me and acting like a father.

The misery of being at Bethany's all night continued throughout the awful day I'd put in at school. Wearing the same clothes I'd slept in, not having showered, and having no breakfast set the stage for a crappy day. We'd missed the bus at Bethany's and her mother dropped us off, swearing at Bethany during the whole ride, not seeming the least bit concerned that some strange kid she hadn't even acknowledged was in the back seat.

Bethany and I had had to sign a late slip at the office and went into second class when it was half over, not impressing Mrs. Taylor in the least. Third class I got assigned a detention for not having my English assignment done. It hardly seemed worth it to tell Ms. Fullerton I'd answered the questions but left them at home.

I'd left all my books home, not bothering to throw them into my backpack before I'd left last night, which made for trouble in every class and with all of my teachers. I'd honestly thought I would be coming back home after winning the little victory of having Dad come and get me. The little victory of making him notice me.

"I was running late myself," I finally answered Jenny.

I ran into the house and straight to the kitchen. I was starving, having had no breakfast and no real lunch. Bethany gave me a toonie, so technically the Mr. Big bar I got from the vending machine was my lunch. I quickly sliced some roast beef and made a sandwich and poured a glass of milk. Someone had plastic-wrapped the meat and stuck it in the fridge.

Mom was nowhere to be seen, and no supper preparations were under way. The same empty kitchen I'd come home to for months gave a good wallop to the hopes I'd had yesterday.

Jenny took the carton of milk from me and poured herself a glass. No sour milk for the precious one. I knew that wasn't her fault, but I felt pissed off anyway, looking at her taking a big swig of milk.

"Dad's bringing supper home," Jenny said. "We have to be at the rink at seven tonight. You like donairs, don't you? Dad couldn't remember if you did or not. I could text him to get you something else if you don't."

That was just making me madder. Of course he couldn't remember. I could have developed a severe allergy or changed my religion since the last time he'd paid any attention to my food preferences. Paid attention to anything about me, really. I considered telling Jenny I was a vegan now and making a big deal out of them not respecting that, even though I was chomping down on roast beef and drinking cow's milk. Why bother? She wouldn't get it.

The phone rang and I looked at the call display. *Gov of NB*. It was probably someone from the high school calling.

"I'll get it," I said, picking up the cordless phone and leaving the room. I stepped out into the garage before hitting Talk.

"Hello," I said, mustering my most mature, parent-sounding voice. "Yes, speaking."

I listened as Ms. Fullerton went into her long explanation of my current failing status, my lack of engagement, and my unfinished assignments. I wasn't sure how well I could pull off a believable mother's response or keep up the disguise of my own voice so I did not answer, which forced Ms. Fullerton to speak again.

"Have I caught you at a bad time, Mrs. Callaghan?"

"Yes."

"I would really like to meet with you and your husband as soon as possible. I am very concerned about your daughter."

"I'll get back to you."

I hung up abruptly before she realized it wasn't Mom.

The garage door slid open just as I was walking up the steps to go back inside. I watched Dad drive in and park his car. Part of me wanted to wait for him to get out of the car and let loose with all the emotions simmering under the surface. But where would I begin? I turned the doorknob, went inside, kicked off my shoes, and headed quickly to my room.

A few minutes later, Dad called me down to the kitchen. I weighed the pros and cons of ignoring his call. Not responding might force him to actually come upstairs and get me. The most obvious con would be if he didn't bother. What if after he called my name a couple of times he just gave up, sat at the table, and ate supper with his other daughter, then went about getting ready for the rink and left without seeing me at all?

I listened, trying to determine if Mom had gone downstairs. She might call my name if I didn't respond to Dad's call. I could have just stayed there to see what transpired. I thought of the part I could play in the family supper scene that was unfolding downstairs. I could take centre stage and ramp the drama right up. Or I could take a more minor role and just be an extra, quietly eating my donair and letting the others play their predictable parts.

Last year I had played a very minor part in the production of *Anne Frank*. When we put the play on for the school, Mike stood up and clapped at my one line, which was embarrassing and also almost made me start laughing, which, given the material, would have been incredibly inappropriate. I had hoped that being in grade eleven would give me a better chance of landing a bigger part, but this year I hadn't even tried out. With my current marks, I would have been kicked out of the cast by now anyway.

"Okay, big brother, I'll go downstairs and wing it. I won't upstage the others."

But supper was uneventful. Not much conversation, except, of course, more talk of the amazing Jenny and her impressive skating techniques. Dad talked a little bit about work. He asked Mom if she'd called district office yet to let them know she was thinking about returning to work. She told him she'd left a message for someone. It seemed at that point Dad was going to check the phone to see if anyone had returned her call. I held my breath, but Jenny didn't mention the phone having rung earlier, and to my relief the conversation moved on.

I didn't have to lie about anything. Nobody asked me any questions that might force me to make something up or to avoid the truth. Jack Nicholson's famous line in the movie *A Few Good Men* came to my mind: "You can't handle the truth." Mike could deliver that line with all the gusto of the original.

As we skirted the truth and avoided talking about anything that mattered, I so wanted to blurt out that line and see what might happen. If even one of us actually told the truth about how we were feeling, it might have been what we all needed. Even if we could just honestly tell each other how hard this was and how much we needed each other, it might have made things better.

Dad and Jenny left, and Mom and I sat in silence as the news showed streams of Syrians crossing the Turkish border, fleeing their war-torn homeland. This scene was playing out on every nightly newscast. Entire families were carrying whatever they could, desperately looking for a safe place to be. I didn't know all the details, but I knew misery when I saw it.

I guessed the misery was more than Mom wanted to see. She pointed the remote, and after scanning the guide, changed the station to *eTalk*. The screen held the rich and the famous on some award-show red carpet with gowns and jewellery that collectively cost more money than a Syrian family would see in a lifetime.

I mumbled, "You can't handle the truth," under my breath as I stood and left the room.

I went into my bedroom and turned on the turntable. I dropped the arm randomly, feeling like Mike would choose the song, and, in some way, tell me something through the music of the band he loved. I turned up the volume to max and sat down on my bed, hugging George of the Jungle close, smelling the T-shirt.

The opening riff moved to the lyrics of the first verse. I squeezed my eyes shut to feel whatever emotion the song gave me.

"Turn that down, Franny."

Opening my eyes, I saw Mom standing in the doorway. I didn't move.

"It's too loud, Franny. Turn it down."

I stared at her, still not getting up. She stood still, too, as if the act of coming across the room and turning the knob was more than she could manage. The chorus began and the drumbeat echoed through the room.

"Franny!"

I stood and lifted the arm.

"It's the new Don't Feed the Wolf album, Mom."

"Don't Feed the Wolf?"

"It was Mike's favourite band. He had all their CDs. They just put out their first vinyl."

"Well, stop playing it so loud."

I wanted to say that by playing the music so loud, I had at least gotten her attention. I wanted to say that Mike picked this song and he was right here with us, but I knew how dumb that sounded and how upset Mom would be if I said something like that. I wanted to just put my arms around her and not have to think of what I should or should not say. I wanted her to be the mother and me to just be some dumb kid who played my music too loud.

"You can put your music back on. Just turn it down a bit, Franny. I'm going to bed."

Of course she was.

# CHAPTER 7

The next day, Dad and Jenny were leaving for British Columbia. Nothing much had changed since they had come home the month before. Mom did go back to work, working three days a week, and that was something, I guess. Most nights we had supper together, but even that hadn't really made the difference I'd hoped it would. The empty place at the table was ignored, just like everything else.

We were getting close to the one-year mark, but nobody was talking about that either. Dad and Jenny were going to be away when the date came. That night, we were going out for supper. Mom and Dad had discussed it the previous night and it struck me how ridiculous it was that they were making a big deal out of our last night together. We'd had a month together, and somehow we'd let those thirty days disappear like smoke.

At least smoke was something you had to react to. You found the source. You made sure whatever was burning was supposed to burn, and if it wasn't, you attempted to put out the fire. You turned your head out of the smoke so it didn't sting your eyes. Smoke was way more tangible than whatever that last month had been in our house.

Supper that night was supposed to be some acknowledgement that it was Mike's birthday as well. That's why Mom was so upset and why it took Dad a while to convince her we should go out to eat.

"I'm not going to a restaurant that puts those silly hats on and sings Happy Birthday to whoever is having a birthday," Mom said.

Mom always used to make a big deal of our birthdays. She always started the day with telling us about when we were born. She never let us forget the part she played in our very existence and the effort it took to bring us into the world. She always recited our time of birth, our birth weight, and several other important facts about the day we came into the world.

"I wouldn't mind going to Deluxe," Mom finally said. "I'll order Mike's favourite. I know you think I'm making too big a deal of all this, but I really don't know how else to do it." Mom was crying by that time and Dad left their room, passing me in the hall without saying a word.

Dad must have realized that for Mom to even agree to go out was a big deal. She'd been going to work all week, and that seemed about all she could pull off. She came home every day and went right to her room. Could Dad not see how much she was struggling leading up to Mike's birthday? Did he not think the weeks leading up to the one-year anniversary of his death would be even more difficult? Wasn't it hard for him, too?

He just seemed to be counting the days until he and Jenny could get out of there. One thing he was for sure not seeing was me. For the whole week, I either hadn't come home after school or went right out after supper. No one even bothered to ask me where I'd been or where I was going.

Every night, I ended up at Bethany's, and we hung out there or went to Sam's or Marin's. Their parents weren't paying much attention to what was going on either. I figured my parents had an excuse—but what excuse did Bethany's mother have for not realizing her daughter was a big-time thief who spent most of her time stoned? And Marin's parents thought she was Little Miss Perfect.

Apparently, Marin had gotten her mother to pay attention long enough to at least get her birth control. Sam's parents were divorced, so she just played them off each other and ended up being able to do whatever she wanted. Somehow, I had been accepted into this group, and I found myself caught up in their dysfunctional social life.

I turned down their invitation that night, though. The Callaghan family was going out to supper. Nothing fancy, but we were all going together. Dad would place our order at the counter and we would sit together in a booth at Deluxe and eat our greasy meal in silence. There would be no cake or singing, but in our own way we would acknowledge the missing person.

Nineteen. Mike would have been nineteen. Legal age. He wasn't much of a drinker as far as I knew, but I'm sure he would have been excited to have the option. He probably would have convinced Mom and Dad to go somewhere that served alcohol.

"Do you have enough tartar sauce, Franny?" Dad asked.

"Here's some ketchup," Jenny said, setting the little white tubs in the middle of the table.

We were all set for condiments and nothing more was said for what seemed like the longest time. I could imagine Mike filling the silence. He would definitely say something gross about the clam bellies. Even though he ate them, he always pulled the clams apart and said something disgusting about them before popping them in his mouth.

I ate, staring at the TV that was mounted on the wall in the corner. I wished I'd sat on the other side of the booth as I watched the news clip showing hundreds of refugees walking along a desert road somewhere in Jordan. Walking to nowhere—or to a somewhere that just held more misery. The next frame showed the refugee camp they were walking toward. This influx of people was headed to the already overcrowded Zaatari camp, which the reporter said held

120,000 people.

Jenny broke the silence and I pretended to listen to what she was saying. I knew it was something about her, something about skating, something about the next few weeks, and I really could not have cared less. I wasn't jealous about any of it except for the fact that she got to leave.

Mike had been so excited to go on the orchestra trip. He fundraised for months. He sat outside the liquor store Saturday after Saturday and actually raised the most money of anyone in the orchestra. It was pretty hard to refuse Mike Callaghan. He had charm that drew people to him.

He was able to pay his whole way and Mom and Dad only gave him some spending money. He texted me that morning saying he was bringing me home something; I never found out what. I just kept thinking afterwards at least the accident was on the way home, so he got to have the week he'd worked so hard for and been so excited about.

It was probably some corny souvenir like the ones he always brought back from other trips: a travel mug that said *Give a hoot—Play the flute* and one that said *Tuba: Play with the big boys*. A T-shirt that said *Face the Music*. A poster saying *Gone Chopin...Bach in five*.

Jenny was still talking. Mom didn't seem to be listening, but Dad was hanging off every word. He seemed just as anxious to get on the road as she was. He could forget about the next few weeks if he was somewhere else.

"Don't Feed the Wolf are coming to Fredericton," I blurted out, interrupting whatever Jenny was saying. "They're the headliner at the May long weekend music festival. This is the band's first time in Atlantic Canada."

Mom looked up from her food. Jenny stopped talking and Dad stood up.

"I need more ketchup," Dad said, walking toward the counter.

"I want to go," I said. I paused, knowing my words were hitting Mom like a ton of bricks. "Some of my friends are going. They're taking the bus up."

I knew as I said the last sentence that I may as well have taken my plastic fork and stuck it in Mom's eye. She stared at me and her eyes began to water. I looked toward Dad, who, even though he had already filled the ketchup cup, appeared to have no intention of returning to the table anytime soon. I looked around the restaurant at other tables, where people were engaged in their own meaningful conversations, or their own frivolous ones.

"I want to go," I stated again, probably louder than necessary.

"Don't be ridiculous," Dad said as he finally sat back down.

Mom bent her head slightly and returned to eating. She picked up a scallop and removed the breading before cutting the white flesh with her plastic knife. I could see tears dripping down her cheeks. She put down her cutlery and picked up a fry in her fingers, dipping it in the ketchup. She set it down, too.

"I'm going to the car," she said as she pushed her tray away and stood up.

I was pouring milk onto my bowl of Shreddies in the dim light of the fluorescent bulb over the stove when Dad came into the kitchen with two suitcases. He set them on the floor by the mudroom door and turned, startled to find me standing in the shadows.

"I thought you were in bed," Dad said. "We're leaving early in the morning."

*Didn't even think you should say good-bye to me?* I put a spoonful of cereal in my mouth, trying not to let any emotion show.

"You know your mother couldn't possibly handle letting you go anywhere on the May long weekend, Franny."

I could feel my anger starting to rise. How dare he tell me what my mother could or could not handle? I'd been the one with her for months. *You come and go—and conveniently always go during the roughest patches. But I couldn't possibly be allowed to go anywhere.*

I poured a few more Shreddies into my bowl and left the kitchen. I waited in the hall for a few seconds, part of me wishing he would follow and say more. Maybe if he tried to comfort me, or at least acknowledge what it meant that I was staying when they got to leave again, I would try to talk to him. I would say how much I missed him, how much I needed him, how much I was hurting.

I could tell him how badly I wanted to see Mike's favourite band. How by seeing them maybe I could get through that terrible weekend. I wouldn't go on a bus if that was the hardest part for Mom to get her head around. I would hitchhike if she thought that would be safer. I would walk, for God's sake, if she didn't want me in a vehicle. Good thing Mike hadn't died in a plane crash, or it would be taking Dad and Jenny a lot longer to get to BC. Why was it okay for *them* to be somewhere on the May long weekend?

The mudroom door opened and the suitcase wheels clicked across the ceramic tile. He wasn't following me. He wasn't even going to say good night or good-bye. Coward.

I headed up the stairs. If they could go, I could, too. I would deal with the fallout later. Nothing I did could make things any worse for Mom. And I was tired of being the only one left behind to care.

# CHAPTER 8

Six days after Dad and Jenny left, Mom told the district office that she wouldn't be back for the rest of the year. Mom started crying openly in front of me. Somehow it seemed easier when she hid behind her bedroom or bathroom door and I saw very little of her.

Even though I worked hard at not allowing myself to cry, I didn't think crying was a bad thing. But I thought healthy crying came along with talking and some sort of mutual comfort being offered. I thought healthy crying stopped and the person carried on somehow. It wasn't that way with Mom.

Mrs. Taylor taught a section on emotional intelligence, and what I saw in Mom didn't look good. She was still barely eating. She was sleeping for hours on end, hardly talking, and showing no interest in anything or anybody. She obviously had depression or PTSD or both, according to what I knew from school and Google.

A little knowledge went a long way, so they said. And knowing what I was seeing was not the same as knowing how to help. All it did was make me feel guilty for being so angry at Mom. Really, I was angriest at Dad and Jenny. It scared me, too, that sometimes I actually felt angry at Mike.

I found myself spending more and more time with Bethany and doing crap I really didn't want to do. One thing I knew for sure was that I didn't want to turn into Mom, so I kept forcing myself out of the house.

The plan that day was to go to the mall with Marin, Sam, and Bethany. I could put in the afternoon there, and if I was careful and made sure I was nowhere near Bethany when she left a store, what trouble could I get myself into?

I had stopped hoping that Mom and her overly protective parenting would kick in and keep me out of trouble. I never appreciated just how good all those rules, curfews, and boundaries were. I used to get so mad when Mom wouldn't let me do something or made me come home way before anyone else. But the previous Saturday, as I'd leaned over the railing of the balcony at Bethany's apartment, puking my guts out, I would have welcomed my mother's intervention. I would have welcomed it more if it had kept me from drinking the four Bacardi Breezers that led to my condition.

Instead I'd gone back inside, washed my face, and slept on Bethany's couch all night, despite the feeling I was being tossed around in a small boat on high waves. I felt even worse in the morning and worse still when I got home after lunch and Mom didn't say a word to me.

"I'm making a box of Kraft Dinner, Mom. Do you want some?"

"No."

"It's really nice out, Mom. You should call Alice and go shopping or something."

"Yeah, right. I wouldn't be good company, and what do I need to shop for?"

"Do you want me to stay home this afternoon? Is there anything you want me to do?"

Mom had always been a big spring-cleaning fanatic and a day like this at the end of April, with the sun streaming through the patio doors covered with all the dirt, grime, and aftermath of the long winter, would have kicked her into high gear. Our chore list would have been a mile long. Mike and Dad would have had the yard looking shipshape and

Mom would have had her garden beds raked, allowing her tulips and crocuses to pop out. As far as I knew, she hadn't even been out in the yard since the last of the snow melted a couple of weeks before.

"Do you want me to do some work in the yard with you, Mom? It is really warm out."

"No, I don't feel like it. You go do whatever you have planned."

I almost lost it, hearing those words. *Go do whatever you have planned.* And to think I'd once thought her letting me do whatever I wanted would be a dream come true. *Be careful what you wish for* was another of Nanny Darrah's lines.

"You should call Aunt Lesley. Have you talked to her lately?"

"She's busy with the kids. She doesn't want to hear me complain. She said as much last time she called."

"I'm sure that's not what she meant, Mom. She's just worried about you."

"Not worried enough to book a flight to come in May. I know it costs a lot of money and she came last year, but…"

I got up and drained the macaroni and started mixing in the cheese. It was weird how Mom acted like she didn't want anyone to bother her, while at the same time becoming angry that nobody was bothering with her. I considered calling Aunt Lesley and telling her just how bad Mom was and asking her to come myself.

But I was tired of being the one to have to figure out how to deal with this. It should have been Dad. I knew he was a grieving parent, too, but his way of handling it seemed to be working better than Mom's. And whether he realized it or not, he still had two children.

I moved my macaroni around my plate, not feeling much like eating. I glanced at the clock and realized that Marin would be there in fifteen minutes to pick me up.

"I'm going to the mall for the afternoon, Mom. My friend is picking me up."

Normally both of those facts would have sent Mom into a tizzy. Wasting my time at the mall on a sunny, Saturday afternoon when inside and outside chores needed to be done would have been enough. And hanging out in the mall with friends was just setting myself up for trouble. Mom had got beaten up in the city when she was a teenager. She went into Saint John on the bus with a friend and they were just minding their own business walking out of the City Market when a girl punched her and stole her purse. She always warned us against being in the wrong place at the wrong time. And, of course, driving with a friend. That would have been out of the question. It wouldn't have mattered to Mom who the friend was.

"Okay," Mom said as she got up from the table. "I'm going up to lie down."

Not even so much as an inquiry as to who I was going with or when I would be home. Nothing.

I forced myself to eat, forced myself not to break into tears. I wanted to follow Mom and tell her not to let me go. *Give me a job to do, Mom. Make me stay home.* I wanted to stop her at her bedroom door and say something that would jar her into doing anything but lie down. I wanted to tell her that Marin was a lousy driver, Bethany was a shoplifter, Sam was the kid I used to come home crying about. My friends were no friends at all. *Don't let me go, Mom!*

I scraped the last of the yellow noodles into the garbage can and threw the plate into the sink. I walked into the mudroom and slipped on my shoes, grabbed my jacket and bag, and went out the door. I'd wait for Marin on the front step. Maybe Mom would look out the window and come to her senses when she saw Marin drive up. The chances were slim but still worth hoping for.

I looked up quickly at Mom's bedroom window a few minutes later as Marin hit the brakes, coming to a jerky stop, one tire up on the sidewalk. The driver's window was down and Marin's extended hand held a cigarette. Upon her sudden stop, she swore loudly. Mom's window was open; maybe she would look out to see who was swearing in her driveway. Bethany put the passenger window down and threw out a Tim Horton's cup. Bad driving, smoking, swearing, and littering. Old Mom would have been on the rampage.

I climbed into the back seat.

For the first hour, we hung out at the food court. I sipped at a large cola and listened to Bethany's plan of attack on the retail establishments she was targeting today. Apparently, she had orders to fill. She'd recruited Sam and Marin to either create a diversion or actually increase the take in a couple of stores. Bethany hadn't asked me to do either, thank goodness.

"I'm buying tickets for Fredericton with my profits and reselling them," Bethany stated. "They're going pretty fast. You want one, don't you, Franny?"

"Yes. I'll give you the money."

"I'm going to get them online for her," Marin said. "My mom is going to put them on her credit card, so you can give me the money. She's going to buy our bus tickets online, too. I'll let you know how much you owe me, Franny."

"Too bad I can't figure out a way to steal the tickets," Bethany added. "I'd try to scam the bus ride, but sneaking all of us on would be a bit of a challenge. Your mom is actually letting you go, Franny? I thought she was a bit of a spaz about stuff like that."

I sucked the last few drops of liquid from the bottom of my cup, trying not to react to Bethany's words. Sure, she used to be a bit of a spaz, if that's what being a mother who gave a damn was. It would be a welcome change from what Mom was right now. Apparently, the other mothers pretty much turned a blind eye to what their daughters were doing. The blind eye Mom was turning these days had nothing to do with her not caring what her daughter was doing. It was more to do with her not caring much about anything at all.

"I've got to go to the drugstore for some stuff," I said, anxious to remove myself from the conversation and the company.

"You on the rag?" Bethany asked.

"Yeah. I have to go to a couple of other stores, too. I'll meet you back here. What time will you guys be done?"

"We don't want to hang around once we're done our business. Meet us at Marin's car in half an hour."

I looked at my phone to register the time as I headed to Lawton's. Thirty more minutes of this and I would be on my way home.

I stood in the Feminine Hygiene aisle and looked at the products in front of me. This was not something I'd ever needed to do until now. Mom's stash of every possible product used to fill one whole shelf in the linen closet. It was hard to believe that Mom's plethora of pads, tampons, panty liners, and menstruation-related paraphernalia could be depleted, but with three of us using it for almost a year and nobody replenishing it, the supply had finally dried up. I'd emptied the last tampon box and stocked my purse with the last two pads before leaving the house this afternoon.

I looked carefully at the prices of the items in my basket and counted my money. Dad had left me some spending money, but it was disappearing fast. I put the Midol back. I would just have to suffer through.

After paying, I made my way to the shoe store. I wasn't buying anything, but I wanted to price a new pair of Birkenstocks. Maybe I would ask for a pair for my birthday. I walked quickly by the game store that was always Mike's favourite place to go whenever we came to the mall. I could almost picture him at the counter, talking gaming with the geeky guy who worked there. I hoped Bethany wasn't hitting that store. I would hate to think of that guy getting his pay docked if inventory went missing.

I was to meet the girls at Marin's car in ten minutes. I tried on a pair of sneakers and jotted down the price of the Birkenstocks I liked.

As I was walking by the food court on my way to the parking lot, I saw Ron and Alice Dixon sitting at a table in the Tim Horton's section. I waved and kept walking.

I walked right to where I knew Marin was parked, in the general area Mom always parked whenever we came to the mall. Mom always tried for a pull-through. Marin had driven into an end parking spot. End spot on the fourth row over from the outside wall of Sobeys.

Instead of Marin's mother's red Passat, there was now a silver Corolla parked there. Maybe I'd miscounted. I scanned the row behind and the row in front, but Marin was not parked in either. I checked my watch. It was actually a couple of minutes before we had agreed to meet. I looked toward the mall entrance, hoping to see the girls walking out the door. I stood there foolishly, not sure what to do next. Had they left without me?

I walked up and down the rows all the way over to the Toys R Us entrance. The whole time I kept scanning the parking lot in case they were driving around looking for me. Marin's mother's car was definitely not anywhere.

I gave up and walked back into the mall. Maybe the Dixons would still be at Tim Horton's and I could ask them for a drive home. The girls leaving in such a hurry and not waiting for me probably had something to do with the shoplifting. Had they run out of the mall to keep from getting caught?

When I got back inside, Alice Dixon was just standing to put her jacket on. It was embarrassing to admit that my so-called friends had left without me, but what else could I say?

"Of course we'll give you a drive home," Alice said. "Ron's had his fill of shopping anyway. Funny they would leave without you."

"Yeah. I must have misunderstood the plan. They probably

thought I was getting a drive with someone else."

"Was it your friend Tara? I thought I saw her mother in Sears earlier."

"No, they were some other friends. I don't think you know them."

I was really glad it was the Dixons I ran into and not Tara or her mother. To have to admit to Tara that Bethany, Sam, and Marin had left without me would have been embarrassing. I knew by the way she looked at me at school sometimes what she thought about me hanging out with those three. Her mother probably would have given me a lecture as well.

A lecture would be a welcome thing at this point, but I wanted it to come from my own mother.

"Are your dad and Jenny away again?" Ron asked. "I was talking to him a couple of weeks ago. She's doing really well, he told me. Pretty exciting if she qualifies for the Commonwealth Games, eh?"

"Yeah, pretty exciting."

Alice seemed to sense my lack of enthusiasm. "What about you, dear? What have you been up to?"

*Drinking, failing at school, hanging out with losers.* "Not much," I answered.

"Oh, I'm sure you've been busy doing all kinds of interesting things. We're parked at the other end of the mall. I just have to stop into Lawton's and pick up a prescription on our way," Alice said.

"I'll go get the prescription," Ron said. "You take the keys, dear, and you and Franny can have a good chat and do some catching up."

On the way to the car, Alice filled me in on everything her two grandchildren were doing. Laura was teaching again and both the kids were in school already. Alice's son, Thomas, and his wife were expecting a baby in June.

"Enough about me," Alice said as she pushed the button to unlock the car doors. "Tell me how things really are at your house. I haven't even seen your mom outside, and she usually can't wait to get into her garden when the weather starts to warm up. I know the month ahead is going to be a tough one."

I was glad to take my place in the seat behind Alice so that she couldn't see my eyes filling with tears. I wanted so badly to let it fly. I wanted to tell her how worried I was about Mom. How lonely I was. How angry I felt.

"She's okay. She was back to work, but since Dad left she hasn't felt up to it. Lots of flu going around. Maybe it's that."

"It's a terrible thing to lose a child. I can't even imagine what your mother's going through. It's hard for all of you. I can't believe he's gone myself. Sometimes I see a young fellow walk by and I think for a moment it's Mike and then I remember. We all miss him, dear."

I was glad to see Ron walking toward the car so I wouldn't have to respond. I was so tired of hearing how hard it was for a parent to lose a child. I knew that, but how come no one ever bothered to mention how hard it was to lose a sibling? I had had a big brother for fifteen years, and then all of a sudden I didn't. I didn't want anyone to feel sorry for me; I just wanted someone to say *I know how hard it is to lose a brother*.

"Do you know how much that prescription would have been if we didn't have coverage?" Ron said as he slid into the driver's seat.

# CHAPTER 9

Bethany texted me later explaining their quick getaway, and my theory was right on. Apparently, Sam had been spotted stealing a shirt in RW&CO, and when confronted by the salesgirl, she took off out of the store. Marin and Bethany were waiting on a bench nearby and the three of them ran out the nearest door and all the way around the building, then jumped in the car and drove out of the parking lot as fast as they could.

The text didn't offer an apology or ask how I got home. I hadn't replied and I hadn't spoken to any of them since. It was a long, miserable, lonely week at school, and on Thursday I almost went over to talk to Tara in the cafeteria.

The previous night, lying in bed, I'd picked up the phone to call Tara. I almost hit the speed dial, which still had her number recorded, but then I remembered what she'd said to me.

"God, Franny, you're not the only one with problems."

It didn't seem so bad now. At the time, though, it had hurt my feelings and pissed me off. What did Tara know about problems? The worst thing she'd faced was when her cat died, and Taffy had been ancient, could hardly walk, and had disgusting, goopy eye sores.

I hadn't expected her to treat me like I was the only one with problems. I just wanted her to understand how hard it was, how sad I was. I wanted someone to just let me cry, just let me feel sorry for myself if I wanted to. Was that what Mom wanted? But here she was, almost a year later, still just wanting to be left alone to feel sorry for herself. Where was that getting her?

Instead of calling Tara, I'd opened my laptop and begun an email to Aunt Lesley.

I was going to meet up with Bethany and Marin with money for my Don't Feed the Wolf tickets and my bus fare to and from Fredericton. I didn't trust them and I wasn't looking forward to hanging out with them during the long weekend, but I had every intention of going to see Mike's favourite band.

I wasn't going to tell Mom I was going, but just before I left I would send an email to Aunt Lesley and tell her. That way, she could call Mom and tell her where I was and that I was fine. That was, of course, if Mom even noticed me missing before Aunt Lesley called her. Either way, I would not put Mom through not knowing where I was on what I knew would be a very difficult weekend for her. Aunt Lesley could explain to her why I had to go and when I would be home.

I would give Aunt Lesley all the details of my weekend away, tell her how I was feeling and how Mom was doing. It felt like a huge weight was being lifted when I began typing. Maybe being totally open and honest with Aunt Lesley would help.

Once I sent the email to Aunt Lesley, there would be no turning back. Once I gave Marin my money, I wouldn't change my mind either. Oh, how I wished that just by hearing Mike's favourite band playing live, I could make Mike alive again. Oh, how I wished it were this time last year and we could change the reality we lived with every day. Oh, how I wished.

I met Bethany at Marin's and gave them the money. Bethany made a big deal of the fantastic price she was giving me. That girl should definitely go into sales.

"I can give you your concert ticket for fifty bucks. It's been a very lucrative week, and I gave Marin's mom the money for the best tickets, but I can give you a deal. After all, we did ditch you at the mall. The bus fare is close to a hundred bucks, though."

I had $200 with me and was glad I only needed to give them $150. I would replace the money I'd taken out of Mom's bank account when I got my birthday money in June. I did not feel the least bit guilty, considering the amount of money Dad was spending on Jenny these days.

I only hung out at Marin's for a few minutes. I wasn't usually up early on a Saturday, and I didn't know what I was going to do with the rest of my day, but I had no interest in going anywhere with Sam and Bethany. They were heading to the liquor store, hoping to con someone into getting them alcohol for a party Max Davis was having at his house that night.

I wasn't wasting my money or my time on that. I would save the $50 for Fredericton. I would get through these next two weeks just going to school and going home. I'd walked to Marin's, which took me about an hour, and was now walking back home again. I wasn't minding the walk at all.

I thought back to Mike's birthday, when we'd eaten at Deluxe. Since that night, I'd seen more newscasts showing refugees walking. Some walked to bodies of water and then got on overcrowded boats. Just about every night, the news told stories of people drowning or boats capsizing. How desperate those refugees must have been to take such risks!

Walking and walking. Imagine leaving your home and the life you knew to just start walking, not having any idea what you were walking toward. Whole families with all they could carry on their backs. Mothers carrying babies, toddlers and older kids walking behind. I had no idea what that would be like. Even days when there was next to nothing in the house to eat, I knew I would not starve. I had running water and a roof over my head.

*God, Franny. You're not the only one with problems.*

I walked by the brick wall at the entrance to Tara's subdivision. So many times, we'd biked out that street and up to the convenience store on Vincent Road. We thought we were so grown up the first time her mom let us do that alone. The lady at the store filled small paper bags with candy, and afterwards we biked to the playground, propped up our bikes against the fence, and sat on the grass. Some bigger kids kicked a soccer ball toward us and told us to move. They swore at us and threatened to take our candy.

I could have walked to the top of the hill and taken the shortcut to Tara's street. I wondered what she would think if I showed up at her house. She was probably still sleeping. What would I say to her parents if they answered the door? "Just passing by, thought I'd stop in"? I hadn't been to their house for five months and one day.

My departure had been a bit dramatic. Tara had followed me out the door after I grabbed my backpack. I was bawling and she was saying over and over that she was sorry. Her dad was still in his dorky pajamas but asked if I wanted him to drive me home. I said I would walk.

When I got home that day there was a message on the phone from Tara's mom explaining to Mom that Tara and I had had a bit of an upset. A bit of an upset. An upset that had kept us from even speaking ever since.

Tara had texted me several times that day. She came up to me at school for a couple of weeks trying to talk to me, but I walked away every time. Mom hadn't even heard the message Tara's Mom left. I'd erased it when I got home. And Mom had never once asked me about Tara in all the months since.

I was surprised to see Alice Dixon sitting at the kitchen table with Mom when I walked in the door. A basket of blueberry muffins sat on the table and Mom and Alice were drinking tea. This used to be a common sight, but I hadn't seen it for a long time.

"You're out and about bright and early, Franny," Alice said. "My kids used to sleep past noon on Saturdays when they were teenagers."

I opened the fridge door and got out the water pitcher, pouring myself a tall glass.

"Have a muffin, dear," Alice said. "Your mom and I are having a lovely chat."

I imagined the lovely chat had been completely one-sided. Mom took a sip of tea, not even bothering to ask me where I'd been. She was not dressed and I was surprised she'd even heard Alice at the door.

"We were happy to see Franny last week when we gave her a drive home from the mall. Terrible we have to run into our neighbours at the mall, though. Don't know where the time goes. The weeks and months go by so fast. Since Ron and I retired, we seem to have less time than we ever did. It's the damn Internet and Netflix, I think. I've wanted to get over, so this morning I just said to Ron, 'I'm going to make muffins and go over for a visit with Marilyn.' I left a couple for Ron. You know how he loves his sweets. He's put on a few pounds since retiring, that's for sure."

I could tell by Alice's nonstop nervous prattle that I'd been right about the one-sidedness of the conversation. Mom was barely acknowledging Alice's words. She'd only taken a nibble of the muffin sitting in front of her. I got up to offer Alice some hot tea.

"I thought Ron looked good the other day. I see him out walking quite a bit," I said.

"Yes, he does try to walk every day, and the kids gave him one of those exercise machines for Christmas. I use it more for a clothes rack than he does for exercise. He even bought a gym membership, but he's not getting his money's worth for that, I don't think. When will Doug and Jenny be home, Marilyn?"

"I don't know exactly, but I do know they won't be home

for the twenty-first. He probably doesn't even realize what the twenty-first is. Seems I'm the only one who cares." Tears were streaming down Mom's cheeks. Alice picked up a napkin and passed it to her. I set down the teapot and put my hand on Mom's shoulder.

"That's not true, Mom."

"He doesn't even want me to put a memorial in the paper, but I am anyway. Fine for him. He gets to leave and forget. We stay here and remember."

"Of course we do. And they do too, Mom."

"Nobody forgets, Marilyn. Nobody forgets your boy." Alice stood to hug Mom, but at the same time Mom pushed back her chair and stood up.

"I'm not feeling well, Alice. Thank you for coming over, but I need to go lie down."

Without waiting for a response, Mom turned and left the kitchen quickly.

"I'm sorry," I said. "You're lucky she even answered the door. She doesn't mean to be rude."

"Oh, sweetie. That's fine. I knew she wasn't doing so well. I never see her outside, and Mrs. McEachern told me she has called several times and gets no answer. Are you okay?"

"I'm fine." I took the paper off my second muffin, trying desperately to conceal how I truly felt.

"Is there anything I can do?"

"Just keep trying. Most of her friends don't even bother anymore. I can't really blame them, but, somehow, I think if they didn't give up and just kept making Mom do stuff, she would get better. She can be nasty, though. She just wants to be alone. She's in bed most of the time."

"I feel terrible I haven't been around more."

"No, don't. It was really nice of you to come by this morning. I don't expect everyone to drop everything in their own lives to try to help us. God, my own father and sister don't bother to stick around."

I got up from the table, picked up Mom's teacup, and put it in the dishwasher. I had said too much. It wasn't fair to burden the neighbours with our problems.

"Laura asks me all the time how you're doing, Franny. Maybe you could message her or call her on the phone. She wouldn't mind at all and would be happy to hear from you."

"Maybe I will. That's one of the hardest parts of all this. Finding someone to talk to who just lets you vent and doesn't try to fix you or humour you or... I don't know. It just gets to be too much. You would think after almost a year it would get easier, but it doesn't."

"Did I ever tell you I lost a sister when I was eleven? She drowned. It was the hardest thing. I still can feel it when it gets close to Labour Day. We were at my aunt's summer cottage for the long weekend. My mother never forgave herself. She'd let Winnie go fishing with my uncle. He drowned, too. Things were never the same. And back in those days, people didn't talk about things the way they do nowadays."

"People don't always talk these days either."

"Maybe when your dad gets back you should suggest some counselling for everybody."

"Yeah. I'll do that. Thank you, Alice."

"Don't thank me. I better get over and get lunch. I will be back, though. I'm going to make a point of coming over to see your mother every day. Even if I just check in for a minute or so, I want her to know she's not facing this anniversary alone."

"Thank you." Part of me wanted to blurt out my plan to go to Fredericton on the long weekend. I didn't want to tell her so she would stop me; I just wanted to tell someone who might care, someone who could give me advice or maybe even figure out a better way to do what I was so determined to do. I wanted an adult to be my safety net if a weekend with my untrustworthy, sketchy friends went badly. It would have been nice to have someone I could call to come and get me if I ended up at the police station.

I was probably being overly dramatic. I would take the bus to Fredericton, go right to the concert site, stay Saturday night in a tent at Mactaquac, and then catch the bus back home on Sunday. I would be fine. The most important part was seeing Mike's favourite band. Mike would look out for me.

Alice came over and gave me a big hug. "I raised four teenagers, you know. This is the hardest time to be missing a parent, and Franny, you're missing both of yours right now. It's not your fault, and things will get better. I'm here for you if you need me. I mean that. Anytime. You can call me anytime. Your parents would have done the same for my kids."

Alice walked over to the computer desk and picked up a pen. She came back to the table and ripped a corner of the napkin in the basket of muffins.

"Here's my home phone and my cell number. You call me anytime, day or night, if you need me. I mean it, Franny."

I took the piece of napkin from her. "Thank you" was all I could muster without totally losing it.

Around four in the afternoon, the doorbell rang. I opened the door to a delivery man holding a flower arrangement.

I hadn't even remembered that the next day was Mother's Day, but apparently Dad and Jenny had. I took the flowers from the man, trying hard not to show the anger I felt. They were sending flowers as if that was enough to get Mom through the first Mother's Day she had to face without her oldest child, the one who made her a mother for the first time. Did Dad really think making a call, giving his credit card number, and having a bunch of flowers in a lovely vase with a big "Happy Mother's Day" banner wrapped around it was enough to get his wife through tomorrow?

# CHAPTER 10

*You never said I'm leaving*
*You never said good-bye*
*You were gone before we knew it*
*And only God knows why.*
*In life, I loved you dearly*
*In death, I love you still*
*In my heart, I hold a place*
*That only you can fill.*

Mom had gotten up early and walked to the end of the driveway in her housecoat to get the paper, oblivious to the weather. She passed me on the stairs, her hair wet from the rain as I was coming down for breakfast. She was clutching the blue plastic-wrapped newspaper as if it were a precious gift she'd travelled a great distance for.

The memorial was cut from the paper and sitting on the kitchen table when I got home from school. She'd chosen one of my favourite photographs of Mike and put it in the paper with the poem. It had been taken the day of his first cello recital.

The poem was beautiful, but it made me so mad. Just the last line, really, because of how true the *only* part was. For the last two weeks, I had tried so hard to get Mom to see me. I was one of the two children she still had and the only child who was here every day. I didn't want to fill the place Mike left; I just wanted to know there was still a place for me.

The trip to Fredericton was all Bethany, Sam, and Marin had talked about all day. We were going to meet at ten in the morning at the Irving on the west side to catch the bus. Marin's Mom was driving us in. Max and two of his friends were going to meet us there. Ethan Rogers was one of them. I didn't know why he was still hanging out with guys in high school.

I felt a bit sick to my stomach when I thought about going, but then there was the part of me that couldn't wait to get to the concert. I'd been listening to all Mike's old CDs and the album over and over. Mike would have been so excited to see them live. I wasn't going to let anything ruin the concert for me.

Sam didn't even know anything about Don't Feed the Wolf. In the cafeteria, she had asked what kind of music Don't Feed the Beaver played. Max made a crude remark, and everyone laughed, making me even more uncomfortable about the prospect of hanging out with them. None of them really cared about the band. They just wanted to party all weekend.

Mom walked into the kitchen.

"Did you see Mike's memorial, Franny?"

"Yes, Mom. It's very nice."

"I'm going to walk to the graveyard. Do you want to come?"

"Sure. Did Dad call today yet?"

I was not quite sure what it was about standing in front of Mike's headstone that comforted me. I didn't go very often, and I preferred going alone, but even while standing there with Mom sobbing, I felt like it was a place I could see Mike. At first, when there was just a rectangle of dirt, it had been awful to go to the graveyard. It was not the least bit comforting standing in the spot where I knew his body was buried. We'd all picked out his headstone together. I asked if they could add "brother of Franny and Jenny." I thought it was important that the fact he was a brother be on the stone, not just that he was the son of Marilyn and Douglas. We looked at a lot of pictures, but somehow, we all agreed on one.

Now it seemed like part of Mike was there when we came. Sounds creepy and macabre, but until the headstone was there, it had felt like we had forgotten him. I hated the thought of winter coming and deep snow covering his spot without a marker there, so I was glad when the headstone was put in place in November.

"I can't believe he's been gone for a whole year," Mom said when her sobbing lessened.

"I know. I miss him so much."

She started walking away. I wanted to tell Mike I was going to the concert and in my mind and heart I would be taking him with me. I wanted to get some reassurance that he would watch out for me. I didn't need to be standing here to have that conversation but was reluctant to leave without having it. I slipped the folded Don't Feed the Wolf poster out of my pocket and knelt to tuck it between the granite monument and the grass. I touched the headstone, silently saying good-bye before following Mom out of the graveyard.

I reread the long email I was ready to send to Aunt Lesley. It hadn't changed much from what I'd originally written. Mom's behaviour in the past couple of days had just reinforced the need for someone to intervene and make this family face how things really were. I was actually worried that if something wasn't done soon to get Mom some help, we would be grieving more than one family member. She seemed to care less and less about everything, including whether she lived or died.

Maybe I was overreacting, but I was going to let someone else determine that. I was tired of being the adult in this house. The next morning I would send it and be on my way, letting Aunt Lesley figure out what needed to be done.

I put Don't Feed the Wolf's first CD in the player and hit

shuffle. Mike's favourite song came on, and as the guitar riff hit my ears, I knew it was Mike telling me I was doing the right thing.

I could hear his voice singing along to the lyrics, *"The road we take can lead us home."* I was taking a road leading me away from home, but one of the reasons I was taking it was so that there was a home to come back to. My trip to the concert and back was going to force my parents to find their way back to being here again. I knew Mike would help me.

I ran out the door and jumped into Marin's mother's car. Before heading downstairs I looked in on Mom, but she was still sound asleep. I was relieved but at the same time slightly disappointed. She'd hardly spoken to me after we came back from the graveyard yesterday. When Dad had called last night, I almost blurted out my plans to him. He couldn't have stopped me from British Columbia, but part of me wanted him to at least realize that him simply stating I couldn't go was not going to change my mind.

"How is your mother doing?" Mrs. Donavan asked as I buckled my seatbelt.

"She's good."

"Now, Marin," she continued, "I expect you to text me when you get to Fredericton. Dad and I will be at the cottage, but the reception is better there since the new tower. One of us will pick you girls up on Monday. Try to stay out of trouble?"

I couldn't believe that was all Marin was getting. My mom wouldn't have let me go in the first place, but if by some miracle she'd consented, she would have had a string of dos and don'ts a mile long. Everything from "Lay toilet paper on the rim of the porta-potty seats" to "Make sure you know where the first-aid tent is." As I imagined my mother's warnings and reminders, I almost chuckled out loud. Better than weeping at my total lack of parental guidance.

When we pulled into the Irving parking lot, I could see Max, Ethan, and Jon Reed standing against the wall, smoking. I wondered if Mrs. Donavan even knew that the boys were going with us. If she did, she didn't offer any other advice to her daughter. If she'd known what a jerk Max Davis was, she would have been concerned with her daughter's involvement with him.

"Just let us out here, Mom," Marin barked impatiently. "You don't have to wait until the bus comes. And where's my spending money?"

Mrs. Donavan passed Marin a hundred-dollar bill, and without so much as a thank you, Marin was out of the front seat, slamming the car door behind her.

*"Get back here and give me a hug, Franny Callaghan, and some manners please!"*

Now I was even imagining my mother's dialogue. I was losing it for sure. I thought of the suggestion Alice made. A counsellor would have a field day with me.

It was Mike's voice I heard next as we left the car and walked over to where the guys were standing.

*"I'm on you, Rogers, like white on rice. Don't even think about laying a hand on my little sister."*

The Maritime Bus pulled into the parking lot. Bethany cursed and stubbed out the cigarette she'd just lit.

"The bus stops in Welsford. You can finish your smoke then," Max offered as he picked up his backpack and headed toward the bus.

I managed to get a seat by myself. Thankfully I wouldn't have to listen to the people I was travelling with. I wasn't looking forward to spending time with any of them. If I could have, I would have just come alone, but hanging out with this bunch was a hardship I was willing to put up with for the sake of seeing Mike's band.

I imagined how crazy they'd think I was if I said I was going to the concert to see my dead brother. I mean, I knew I wasn't going to *see* him, but I was confident that I would feel him there beside me. I let my mind wander to the fantasy of him and me travelling on this bus together or even possibly having Dad's jeep and going to hear Don't Feed the Wolf on this May long weekend...if last year's May long weekend had never happened.

From that, my mind wandered to imagining Aunt Lesley reading the email. Would she call Mom right away or wait a while, not wanting to upset her? She would probably tell Uncle Craig first and maybe discuss the possibility of flying to New Brunswick. I told her that Mom needed someone to force her to get some help. Would she call Dad and discuss what I'd written with him? Would he be surprised by the things I'd said? Would he come right home?

I felt completely overwhelmed by my thoughts and tried to make myself more comfortable, hoping the rhythm of the bus would lull me to sleep. Mom certainly had perfected the art of using sleep as an escape. I closed my eyes.

Max's loud voice and his bumping the back of my seat woke me up. I wasn't sure how long I'd been sleeping or where I was.

"Do have any smokes, Bethany?"

"In my backpack under the seat."

I kept my eyes shut, hoping to get back to sleep. I heard Max open the zipper of the backpack.

"What's this? Lego?" Max asked.

"It's a Christmas ornament."

"Neat. Where'd you get it? I used to love Lego. Give you five bucks for it."

"No friggin' way. It's got sentimental attachment for me."

"I'll give you ten bucks. You'll sell anything if the price is right."

"Not that. It means too much to me. It was the last thing my dad gave me before he died."

I couldn't believe what I was hearing. Not only was Bethany claiming the ornament was hers, she was making up a whole sad story to go along with it. As far as I knew, she never even knew who her Dad was, let alone had some touching memory about an object he gave her before he died. I could feel my rage building, but instead of jumping up and confronting her lie, I just squeezed my closed eyes tighter, feeling more miserable than I had since getting in Marin's mother's car.

This so-called friend of mine had not only stolen Mike's ornament and then denied it, she had no trouble lying about it and claiming it as her own—even with me sitting in the seat right in front of her. She had no loyalty or honesty. None of these people cared the least bit about me and sure as hell didn't care what this weekend meant for me.

I wished I'd called Tara. She would have tried her best to understand and help me get through this weekend. She may have even come up with a plan to get us to the Don't Feed the Wolf concert together. I would have been able to tell *her* why going meant so much to me.

The bus pulled into the Irving parking lot in Welsford. I turned my head, trying to stop the shaking and stuff down the feeling of nausea. I kept pretending to be asleep as the others filed past me on their way out of the bus.

In Fredericton, we took taxis to the gates of Mactaquac Provincial Park. The concert site was directly across the road from the campground. We were going to set up our tents at our campsite, and then make our way to the large field where the concert would begin around dusk. Our passes meant we could come and go, staying for as many bands as we wanted. The headliner was coming on stage at midnight. I figured my companions would be wasted by then, but I had every intention of being fully present, as close as possible to the stage to take in the band and celebrate the life of one of their biggest fans.

"I'll pay your share of the cab fare," Bethany said matter-of-factly as we got out of the taxi. Possibly she realized that I'd heard her lie to Max about Mike's ornament and was feeling guilty. Before this weekend was over, I hoped I could get enough nerve to confront her about it and demand the Lego ornament back. At least I was quite confident she wasn't going to sell it to the highest bidder. I knew she had a stash of cigarettes, condoms, and other items she planned on getting top dollar for. And I could only imagine what Ethan Rogers had for sale.

We pitched two tents at the campsite. I was glad there would be a tent for the girls and a tent for the boys. It did concern me a bit, though, which of the two tents Max and Marin would decide to hole up in. I had no doubt what they'd be doing all weekend. I would just do my best to avoid being around to witness it. My plan was to stay at the concert, possibly sleeping under the stars, as the weekend weather was supposed to be clear and warm.

A driving rainstorm had caused the bus to leave the road somewhere in Quebec last May 21. It rolled several times as it plunged down a deep bank and settled in a ravine. I'd only seen a picture of the broken guardrail on the news, but the picture in my head of the scene was vivid enough. Apparently, recovering the bodies and rescuing the injured had been very difficult. Luggage and musical instruments were strewn all over the accident site.

No charges were laid, but an inquiry came up with forty-five recommendations, one of them that night travel be avoided.

Sam passed me a sandwich from a huge rolling cooler full of food her mom had sent with her.

"Want a beer?" Max asked.

"No, not right now, thanks," I answered. I had no intention of drinking all day, but from the looks of it I was the only one who wasn't. Marin was already halfway through her second Mike's Hard Lemonade. Just seeing his name on the bottle was hard enough for me. I certainly didn't need the melancholy or downright despair I would have felt after drinking a couple of them. No, I was going to stay clearheaded and completely in control of my emotions.

The chicken salad sandwich was delicious. It reminded me of the sandwiches someone had brought to the house after the funeral. I'd felt so guilty enjoying the huge spread of food afterwards. It seemed so wrong to be eating and chatting like it was some sort of party. Even Mom had rallied to put on the appearance of the perfect hostess until she hit the wall around midnight. It was as if a fuse blew or her battery died. She went from fully engaged to a mass of jelly that Aunt Lesley needed to help upstairs, get undressed, and put to bed.

The six of us walked out of the campground and across the road to get our bracelets. There were already throngs of people streaming onto the concert site. It put me in mind of the news coverage of refugee camps. The camps were much larger, of course, and the masses of people much larger as well. And this crowd was mainly young people, not the range of ages from infants to the elderly who descended on the makeshift camps trying to find shelter.

The concert site itself looked like a vast field of activity. I could see just past the registration booth the first-aid tent and checked that off in my mind. Porta-potties seemed to be dotted around the outside edges of the field. I could see the stage set up in the distance of what probably once had been a farmer's field. I wondered what would be left after the hordes of music lovers vacated the site, leaving garbage and God knows what else behind. At least it wasn't muddy.

Mike used to watch YouTube videos of Woodstock. He was an expert on the artists who'd performed and the trivia surrounding the event. He had posters and books about the historic festival that took place in the hay field outside the town of Woodstock, New York, in August of 1969. The three-day festival attracted 400,000 people and changed music history.

Mike owned the album featuring artists like Arlo Guthrie,

Jimi Hendrix, The Who, and Joe Cocker, with the iconic photograph showing a hill covered with wet and miserable concertgoers and a couple in the foreground wrapped up in a comforter. This was no Woodstock, but Mike would have been just as enthusiastic about the crowd gathering to listen to the lineup of local bands and the headliner.

Most of these kids wouldn't even have known who Arlo Guthrie was. Mike, a big fan, could recite all eighteen minutes of "Alice's Restaurant." He could sing "Walking Down the Line," too—Bob Dylan's song that Arlo Guthrie covered at Woodstock. He'd sung it at the most inopportune and embarrassing times.

From across the field I could hear the echoes of musicians doing their sound checks. Mike would have been able to identify each instrument and whether or not it was in tune. He would have paid close attention to every aspect of the setting up and the delivery of the music being offered on this sunny afternoon. He would have been perfectly content to find a spot to sit and take it all in. It was always about the music for him. He would have made a name for himself wherever his love of music and his talent led him.

I looked behind me. Bethany was getting her wristband. Everyone else would probably head back to the campsite to drink some more while Bethany stood at the gate selling some suckers her extra tickets for twice what she paid for them. She never missed a chance to "embrace opportunity" and make a few bucks.

I was going to go somewhere and sit on the grass in the warm sunshine of the mid-afternoon and start my time with my brother. My phone had beeped a couple of times as I was walking out of the campsite. I saw that both texts were from Aunt Lesley. Once I settled and talked to Mike in my head a bit, I would text Aunt Lesley back, simply telling her I was fine.

A tall, skinny guy was standing in front of the microphone on the lower stage. I sat where I could see him clearly. He was repeating, "Testing, testing," over and over, and then strapped his guitar over his shoulder. Mike had bought a guitar with his own money and started taking lessons from a guy in Hampton.

"This guy can play the guitar, and even if he couldn't, just his hair makes him a musician," Mike had told me.

I hadn't known what Mike was talking about until the night I went to Hampton with Mike and saw his guitar teacher. The sweep of hair on top of the guy's head was not like anything I'd seen before. Mike called it a pompadour.

"Musicians need a look, Franny. Elvis, Michael Jackson, even Justin Bieber. They have a look. I haven't quite figured mine out yet."

The guy on the stage who was now starting to sing looked like a hundred other guys his age. His plaid shirt and jeans were nothing distinctive either. His voice came through the speaker, and I closed my eyes, letting it resonate.

Mike would say, "If you don't have a look, you need a sound that stops everyone in their tracks."

Mike had been kind. He never said mean things about musicians unless they were the boy bands I used to like. He accused *them* of being fake, a product put together to sell and push like the flavour of the month. Real musicians, whatever type of music they played, deserved respect for simply putting themselves out there. Mike would not have criticized this guy. He would have admired his guitar playing and given him a chance.

I quickly texted Aunt Lesley without reading her two lengthy messages.

*Got to the concert and will text you later.*

I turned off my phone and stuck it in the front pocket of my backpack.

# CHAPTER 11

I didn't know how long I'd been sleeping when I was jarred awake by the sound of the cello. I sat up quickly and stared at a girl sitting on the stage to one side of the trio that was singing. Her familiar body movements and the melodious sound of her instrument brought tears to my eyes.

*"Why is playing the cello like peeing your pants? They both give you a nice warm feeling."*

I got to my feet, smiling with the memory of the joke Mike had always told about the cello. I suddenly realized how badly I needed to pee.

I was just coming out of the porta-potty when I spotted Sam and Bethany heading through the crowd toward me.

"We wondered where you got to," Bethany said. "You're missing a good party. A bunch of Fredericton kids are camping beside us."

"We've already gotten a warning from the park security," Sam continued. "What have you been doing?"

*Listening to music. Spending time with my brother. Crying and feeling the loneliest I've felt all year. Watching a cellist and pretending it was my brother on the stage playing. Blocking out hundreds of people so that I can feel the person I came here to be with.*

"Just hanging out, listening to some of the music and enjoying the sun. I'm going to go grab a hotdog right now."

I walked away, not waiting for them to say anything more about the fun I was missing. If I could ignore the milling crowd, I sure as hell could ignore my drunken companions. If I was lucky, I could hide in this crowd and they wouldn't find me again. I made a mental note to use the porta-potty farthest away from the entrance next time.

I loaded my hotdog with all the fixings. I was much hungrier than I realized and sat down nearby to eat. The crowd was increasing and I could feel the buzz in the air. It was apparent that more than just the group at our campsite was partying. From where I sat I could see and hear lots of evidence of that. Several people wearing white Security shirts were milling about the crowd but obviously not enforcing any underage-drinking laws. Large red solo cups dotted the crowd.

I could smell weed nearby, too. It wasn't even dark yet and the rowdiness of the crowd was already apparent. I could see a large tour bus with "Don't Feed the Wolf" written along the side parked near the entrance. In a few more hours, the band would take the stage and make being in the middle of this chaos worthwhile.

A few minutes later, as if just breathing the secondhand smoke was enough to give me the munchies, I headed toward the snack tent to buy a second hotdog.

*This one's for you, Mike*, I thought as I loaded on the onions. He loved onions.

I returned to where I'd been sitting before eating my second hotdog. The spot was still free, but most of the knoll was now covered with blankets, sleeping bags, backpacks, and lots of kids settling in for the concert to begin. The music was recorded tunes now until the night's sets began.

I took a bite, thinking about how lonely I was. They say you can be lonely in a crowd of people. Sometimes living in large bustling cities, passing thousands of people every day, can be the loneliest of all.

I could see the groups of kids nearby laughing and carrying on with each other; I had no desire to be a part of that. I was perfectly content to be alone in this large crowd. I was lonely because I missed my brother. I'd felt this loneliness every day since the accident. He was with me, but so far away from me, and his absence felt further as each day passed. I knew the act of coming to this concert was not going to change that. As more time passed it would get harder to feel his presence, and I knew that when this concert was over and I went back home his absence would take on a whole new reality. I had heard people say the first year is the hardest, but I was afraid of just how hard the second year was going to be.

I let my mind go to what might be going on at home. I was so hopeful that my departure and my email to Aunt Lesley would change things. Something drastic needed to happen to get us moving into the second year in a healthier way. We needed a plan to bring the family back together so we could find our way to face the life we were forced into when that bus hurtled down the embankment.

I was still by myself when the sun began to set over the far hill. The sunset was amazing, the colours changing like a kaleidoscope as dusk took over. The opening bands brought the crowd to life, and there were dancing, swaying bodies all around me. I would probably have to relocate before Don't Feed the Wolf came on or I was not going to be able to see them at all. But maybe just fading into the background of activity taking in the sound of their familiar songs would be better than squeezing my way down front. I would decide closer to their set.

The girls beside me reminded me of Tara and my old crowd: not trying to be cool, just hanging out together and enjoying each other's company. They were drinking pop. They probably had a parent picking them up at the gate at a predetermined time. I didn't feel as if I needed to try to get to know them, but it felt good knowing they were next to me and that I didn't have to worry about them. On my last trip to the bathroom I'd seen lots of out-of-control drunks. I just missed getting thrown up on as I stood in line to use the porta-potty.

I would try to stay put and not go too far, even though the girls had kept my spot for me last time. It wasn't even dark yet. Once the cover of darkness gave the crowd more anonymity, God knew what would happen. I didn't want to be in the middle of it.

Another thing the darkness would provide was the freedom to sit and cry as Don't Feed the Wolf played the songs that held such emotion for me. In the dark, I could truly give in to the fantasy of having my big brother right beside me. I would figure out later how to get back to the campsite and get through the night and the hours until I could get on the bus and head back home. Mike would help me get back home.

"My name is Morgan. What's yours?"

I was startled. I'd been an arm's length from this girl for hours and we hadn't said a word to each other. She'd nodded a couple of times. It had been her friend who had offered to watch my blanket and save my spot. Another one of the girls had offered me an apple a while back, but I hadn't really talked to any of them.

"Franny."

"You must be quite a music buff to come all by yourself."

"I came with some friends, but I'm not really into the same stuff they're into. I'm just here for the headliner, really."

"Me, too. I convinced my friends to come to the festival once I heard Don't Feed the Wolf was coming. They hadn't even heard of them before. And they're not partiers. You can probably tell we're a bunch of nerds."

"Nothing wrong with that," I said.

"Which album is your favourite? Their new one is amazing but I think the musicality of the first one is better. They lost two of their most talented members and have a different manager and producer now."

I didn't know what to say.

"My brother was the real expert. I just kind of fell into it. I really like them, though."

"Why didn't your brother come?"

"He died. A year ago today, actually."

I had turned away from Morgan before answering and didn't see her face, but I recognized the awkward silence, however brief, that always accompanied my telling anyone about Mike. It never got easier and I expected it never would, but not telling people would never change the truth of it either.

"Oh, I'm so sorry. Being here must be really hard for you."

"Thank you. It is and it isn't. The whole year has been hard." I wasn't sure how much I wanted to tell this stranger, but it did feel good having a conversation and feeling like I had nothing to lose by letting myself open up. "I came for *him*. Mike was the one who loved the band. I just started listening to them."

"Did he have a favourite band member?"

"He loved the guy who played the electric violin. Mike played the cello. He was in an orchestra. He was coming home from an orchestra trip when the accident happened."

"I remember hearing about that accident. It was in Quebec, right? My oldest sister plays the cello, too. She was on stage earlier. She's working with the sound crew. That's the only reason my mom let me come. She knows Stephanie will look after me."

"Mike always looked after me. It used to get on my nerves, but I'd give anything to have him still around to keep an eye on me."

"I'm sure he still is. I believe the people we love never really leave us. He's probably watching out for you right now."

My eyes filled with tears. The compassion in this girl's voice was sincere and I felt the caring in her words—more caring and understanding than I'd gotten from anyone in a very long time. "I came to be with him. When the band starts, I'm going to let the music bring him to me. I wanted to be alone so that I could feel him. The kids I'm with just gave me someone to travel with. They don't have any idea why I'm here."

"I won't keep talking to you and I won't bother you when the band starts playing, but I'm right here if you need me or want someone to talk to. I can't even imagine what it must be like to lose a sibling. He'd be proud of you for coming, you know."

The crowd erupted when Don't Feed the Wolf came onto the stage, but I could hear the familiar sound of the first song above the din. I could picture Mike playing the air guitar to the opening riff and rocking his body to the distinctive rhythm. I knew every word, more from hearing it coming from Mike's room than the months of playing it in my own. I could picture the posters in his room. It was time to decide what to do with Mike's things. Keeping everything in place as if he were coming back was not going to bring him back. He wouldn't have wanted us to keep the things he loved in a closed shrine.

I stood and let the music move me, not the least bit concerned with how it looked to the others around me. It didn't matter what anyone else thought. I could see hundreds of kids dancing and swaying to the music. I looked over at Morgan and her friends, who had linked arms and were moving to the music, too. She turned and smiled at me, knowingly. This was the gift I'd been waiting to receive. I closed my eyes and let myself go.

# CHAPTER 12

The clapping and hollering that prompted the encore quieted and the last song was delivered. The lights dimmed a bit and crew members were emptying the stage. Calm recorded music came through the speakers. There was still an occasional burst of laughter and drunken revelry, but the crowd around me dispersed a bit. I realized how cold and tired I was. I'd thought earlier that I might just curl up and try to sleep in my spot, not bothering to head back across the road to the campsite.

Morgan and her friends packed up their stuff and headed to meet her sister, who would soon be finished her work and ready to drive them home. I wished that someone would take me right home. It would be so nice to sleep in my own bed. Before going to bed, I would go into Mike's room and choose one of his posters and take a couple of his favourite stuffies, which he kept on the top shelf in his closet, nearby but not out in the open—a reminder of the kid he had been. He'd gone through a stage of collecting stuffed woodland creatures: moose, wolves, foxes. I would take one and snuggle up in my own bed with it, relishing the closeness to my big brother that this night brought me. I felt a happiness I'd been longing for and a new belief that there could be more happiness in my future.

I made my way through the much smaller crowd. Lots of kids were huddled together in the cold. Some were passed out or sleeping. Some were still going strong. I wrapped my blanket around my shoulders, careful to hitch up the corners so I wouldn't trip as I walked. I didn't want to stumble and fall onto a pile of sleeping drunks or knock into someone looking for a fight. I could see the lights of the gate in the distance and picked up my pace.

Thoughts of woodland creatures were in my brain and I was a bit nervous about walking through the campground by myself. Nervous of the animals both woodland and human. I was slightly relieved when I saw Ethan standing against the chain-link fence at the road. Maybe he was walking back to the campsite and I could go with him.

"I figured you were still here," Ethan said as I approached him.

"Are any of the others?" I asked.

"No, Bethany passed out hours ago. Sam and John left a while ago and Marin and Max barely came out of the tent all night. Not sure why they even bought concert tickets. The band was good, eh?"

"They were awesome. It went so quickly. I hated when they stopped."

We started walking across the road. Several cars were lined up, parents waiting for their kids, a couple of taxis ready to take drunks back to the city and the comfort of houses. Again I felt a pang, wishing I could sleep in my own bed tonight and process the amazing closeness I felt with my brother.

"Mike loved Don't Feed the Wolf," I blurted.

"I think he was the one who introduced me to them. We used to hang out in grade eight, you know. He was a good guy."

"Yeah, he was."

"I'm really sorry he died."

The park reception centre was in darkness and we had to crawl under the barrier that closed the entrance for the night. We walked in silence on the narrow, paved roadway illuminated with the sliver of moon shining in the clear sky. I could smell the smoke of extinguished campfires. I was glad not to be walking alone, fearful that each of the night noises could be a creature that might jump out at me.

As we approached our campsite I could see three guys, likely the Fredericton kids Sam mentioned earlier, still sitting around a burning fire. They were passing a joint and turned slowly toward us.

"Hey, man," one guy said. "Got any beer left?"

Ethan walked over to the cooler and took out two cans of Alpine, passing one to the guy and one to me.

I sat down and pulled the tab. I would sit and warm myself by the fire, drink this beer, and then figure out which tent I would sleep in if I didn't fall asleep curled up under my blanket on this lounge chair.

Ethan passed me the joint and I took a drag. I was tired and anxious to get the night over with so that morning would come and I could get on my way home.

"We heard the music from here," one of the other guys said. "I told you we didn't need to waste our money buying tickets."

"You might have hooked up if you'd gone over," the third one muttered. He looked toward me. He probably figured Ethan had picked me up at the concert, bringing me back to the campsite like a successful hunter.

"Tanner didn't have to go across the road."

I looked over to a mound on the ground I hadn't noticed when I first sat down. The red plaid double sleeping bag had two heads and naked shoulders sticking out of the top and I saw that one of the heads was Sam's. I didn't know the other one.

"I wasn't touching that Bethany one, that's for sure. She probably would have charged me by the hour. Tom paid her seventy bucks for that ticket."

"He's got more money than brains anyway."

I took another swig of the beer. It didn't taste all that bad, and it was helping me relax. I was exhausted and quite happy to lay there. I was not going to join the conversation these idiots were having. Maybe they would head back to their own campsite soon.

As if they could read my mind, all three got to their feet and without saying a word staggered into the dark onto the neighbouring campsite.

"What was your favourite song?" Ethan asked.

"The first one they played, I think, but I like them all. Did you know they have a new manager and lost two band members since their first album?"

"Yeah. One of the guys plays with Hedley now."

I reached for my backpack and dug in the front pocket for my phone. I turned it on and waited for the screen to light up. I had five messages, all from Aunt Lesley. I scrolled down, not reading any of them but quickly texting a reply.

*Concert over. I'm fine. I'll be home tomorrow.*

I turned the power off again and put the phone back in my backpack.

Ethan passed the joint to me again.

"No, I'm good. I can barely keep my eyes open."

"I've got a pup tent over there. It's got an air mattress and pillows in it. Go ahead and crawl in if you want. I'm going to have another beer and finish smoking this joint."

Ethan got up, put another stick of wood on the fire, and then walked over to the cooler. I stood up, grabbed my backpack and my blanket, and headed for the tent Ethan had pointed to. I was glad not to have to play Russian roulette with the two big tents, possibly ending up squeezed beside Max and Marin. I didn't really want to wake Bethany, either.

"Thanks, Ethan," I said, kicking off my sneakers, unzipping the tent, and crawling in. I slipped off my jacket but left my jeans and shirt on. I stuffed my book bag up to the head of the tent and lay down, covering myself with my blanket, ready for the sleep I knew would come as soon as I closed my eyes.

The bridge from a deep dream state to wakefulness always comes with a bit of a jolt. Maybe I heard the tent zipper. Maybe I felt the pressure of his body as he squirmed in beside me. Maybe I heard his breathing or smelled his sour breath. Maybe it was his words that woke me.

"You wanted this two years ago. You would have got it, too, if your stupid brother hadn't butted in."

I was now wide awake and my mind registered panic, then anger, followed quickly by fear. I shifted my body and knew the narrow tent offered me no escape from the closeness of what I realized was Ethan's naked body. If I made a sound in my panic, it was muffled by a sloppy kiss while his hands grabbed my breasts with a forcefulness that made me wince. My eyes registered only the pitch darkness of the small enclosure.

I reflexively jerked my face away from his, but he grabbed my hair and pulled me closer.

"Oh, please. I knew you wanted it when you got out of Marin's car. That hard-to-get act of yours doesn't fool anybody. You were sure glad to see me waiting for you tonight."

Again I tried to squirm away from him, but his grip on my hair tightened, the pain stabbing my scalp.

I knew nothing I could say was going to change the outcome he had in mind. Probably screaming would get me nowhere. Everybody near enough to hear me was in a drunken or post-sex stupor and wouldn't jump to my defense. Ethan started pawing at my lower body and awkwardly fumbled to unfasten my jeans.

"Stupid, fucking zipper," he muttered.

"Wait a minute. I'll crawl out and take my clothes off."

I couldn't believe how calmly the words came. I prayed that he believed I was totally on board with what he had in mind and wouldn't follow me from the tent to ensure my return. He rolled over slightly, giving my left breast one more squeeze, as if that would seal the deal and hurry me along for the anticipated pleasure he planned on delivering.

The cold air hit me and I quickly fumbled for my sneakers. I found one right away but it took me a few seconds to locate the other one. My heart was racing. I looked around, doing one more assessment of the help I could expect, and made the decision to get as far away from there as quickly as possible. Ethan's nakedness and drunken state were no guarantee he wouldn't come after me. I slipped my sneakers on without taking the time to tie them and started running down the paved track, hoping the direction I'd chosen led to the main road.

I didn't stop until I reached the bend that led to the short roadway out of the park. I leaned against the rail fence and listened for any sound of Ethan coming after me. I didn't hear anything. The fear that had been deep in my throat like thick bile bubbled up and I began to sob. Between sobs I called out my brother's name over and over, as if it could make him swoop in and save me. It echoed through the stillness. "Mike!" I called again and again, in a desperate plea.

How had I fallen for Ethan's smooth, knight-in-shining armour act? He'd pretended to be so concerned, so interested in the band. He actually offered sympathy for my loss. It had all been an act to lull me into the trust he was more than eager to take advantage of. Mike had known the real Ethan Rogers. How could I have let my guard down?

I started walking quickly toward the entrance, still calling Mike's name but more calmly now: "Mike, Mike, Mike," a mantra to steady my shaking, terrified body. In my trancelike state, I almost didn't see him with his back to me, a hooded sweatshirt pulled up, leaning against the entrance gate. My shaking intensified but my fear dispersed. My brother had come to save me.

"Are you okay?" The guy who turned toward me was a complete stranger. His white teeth gleamed in the darkness. I felt no fear, only relief.

I squeezed under the gate and walked toward him. "Yeah, I'm okay now. I had a bit of a situation. But I'm okay."

"How did you know my name?"

"I didn't. Mike's my brother's name. I was calling *him*."

"Is he supposed to be picking you up?"

"No."

"Well, I'm Mike Richards. I'm just waiting for my mom to come get me. I missed my ride and had to call her. I woke her up, so it will take her a while to get here. Hated to do that to her, but couldn't really see myself walking all the way home. We can give you a ride if you need one."

I considered my options. My phone, wallet, and clothes were in the bag I'd left behind. I could ask this guy to walk back with me so I could get it, but I had no desire to see Ethan or tell this guy the details of what had just happened.

"Yeah, I'd take a ride into Fredericton if that's where you're going."

"Yep. We may as well start walking. Mom will see us. That way if the guy—I assume it was a guy that caused your *situation*?—comes along, we'll be gone."

"That would be good. I think he's too drunk to bother, but I'm really glad you were standing here."

A few minutes later, we saw lights heading toward us and Mike's mother's car pulled up. Mike opened the back door and motioned for me to get in.

"Mom, can we give Franny a drive into Fredericton?"

"Of course. Where do you live, Franny?"

"Where do you guys live?"

"We live in Marysville, but I can take you wherever you need to go. You shouldn't be out walking alone in the middle of the night."

I didn't know Fredericton very well and wasn't sure where to tell them to drop me off. I wasn't going to tell them I had nowhere to go.

"Thanks, that would be great. King Street. The corner of King and Regent. I can walk to my aunt's apartment from there. I hope it's not too far out of your way."

"No problem. How was the concert, Mike?"

"It was great, Mom. Sorry I had to call you. I thought Hayden knew I was getting a ride with him, but when I came out he was gone."

I settled into the comfort of the back seat, staring out at the occasional house light as we drove along the highway. Thinking about how close I'd come to being raped, I was almost sick to my stomach.

I shifted my weight, pulling the bills and change out of my jeans pocket. I'd paid for my second hotdog with a twenty-dollar bill and stuffed my change in my pocket, forgetting to transfer it to my wallet. At least I had a little bit of money. But along with my other things, my bus ticket was in my backpack.

Tricia Richards pulled into the parking lot of the King Street Tim Horton's. The clock on her dash said 3:48.

"You're sure this is okay? I can drive you right to your aunt's if you want me to. I really don't mind."

"No, this is great. I'll run in and get her a coffee. She has a new baby and will probably be awake. Thank you so much. I don't know what I would have done if Mike hadn't been standing there."

"You're sure you're okay?" Mike asked.

"Yeah, I'm fine. Thanks again."

I got out and closed the car door, waving to Mike as his mom drove away. I could have told them my predicament. I could have asked to use one of their cell phones to call my mother. I was sure they would have been more than happy to offer whatever help they could, but something kept me from doing that. Embarrassment; shame, maybe. How stupid of me to crawl into Ethan's tent, not realizing he would assume I was offering to have sex with him.

Mike had warned me.

I shivered in the cool early morning air, my short-sleeved T-shirt offering no warmth. I walked quickly into the empty coffee shop.

A woman behind the counter was filling up a coffee pot. I stood a moment, feeling the warm air and taking in the smells. I would order a coffee and a bagel and sit here as long as I could. I needed to figure out a plan.

"A large double-double and a maple French toast bagel, toasted, with butter, please," I asked.

"You're out bright and early, or else out really late," the woman said.

"Yeah."

"Have a seat and I'll bring it over to your table. Sit in front of the fireplace. You look half frozen."

This grey-haired woman looked like she could be someone's grandmother and certainly seemed to have caring and grandmotherly concern for the poor girl who just wandered in looking like she'd escaped from somewhere. No jacket, no handbag or backpack, and, probably the most obvious of all these days, no phone in her hand.

I probably could find my way to the spot where the bus let us off. I was pretty sure we were supposed to catch it at the same place at noon. Maybe one of them would find my backpack when they packed up and bring it with them. I wondered what Ethan would say to explain my absence. He wasn't likely to say I ran away before he could rape me. He probably wouldn't even have considered it rape.

I felt sick thinking what would have happened if I hadn't tricked him. And what if I'd slipped off my jeans before covering up to go to sleep? I couldn't have fought him off.

I felt even more nauseated thinking of seeing him get on the bus acting like nothing happened. I didn't want to see any of them. The grey-haired woman interrupted my train of thought as she set down my coffee and bagel on the table in front of me.

"Are you all right, dear?" she asked.

"I'm fine, thank you."

"You can sit here as long as you need to. We don't get busy until around six. It will be pretty quiet until then. Amira and Miriam will be in soon. Amira sweeps the floors and empties the garbage cans. She walks her mother to work every day and earns a bit of pocket money by helping clean up." She paused. "What they have been through, I can't even imagine. Amira speaks English quite well. Don't be afraid to talk to her. It annoys me how some people think these poor Syrians are monsters just because they are Muslim. You'd be surprised what some customers say. Miriam's the best cook we've had since I started working here, I'll tell you that."

I took a swig of the hot coffee. This woman reminded me a bit of Mrs. Reynolds. I could probably confide in her and even ask to use the phone. I thought of the piece of napkin in my jeans pocket. Something had made me stick it in there just before leaving my bedroom yesterday. I could call Alice. I know she and Ron would come to get me.

I heard an unfamiliar language and turned to see two women walking through the door. The youngest appeared to be around my age and the older possibly a year or two older than Mom. This must be Amira and her mother. The mother embraced the girl and kissed both her cheeks. She said something that from her body language appeared to be an instruction of some kind. The girl kissed her mother back and released herself from the embrace. The parting seemed more serious and difficult than the situation warranted. The older woman, from what I understood, was just going to work in the kitchen a few feet away and the younger was going to begin sweeping. The emotion was as if they were parting for a long and unpredictable journey.

I turned my head quickly when they parted and the girl turned to face me. I realized I'd been staring at them like they were on TV, not a few feet away from me. I took a bite of my bagel and tried to appear uninterested.

Amira began putting the chairs upside down on the tables.

When she finished the last table, she walked down the hall, returning with a broom and dustpan.

"Hello," I said timidly.

"Hello."

She began sweeping in the farthest corner from where I was sitting. I finished my bagel and took the last drink of coffee. I stood up to put my dishes on the counter. I walked over and took a chair down from a table in the area she'd already swept.

"I'll put the chairs back down for you." I said.

She smiled. "Thank you."

"Your mother is very beautiful."

"Thank you."

"How long have you been in Canada?"

"Eighty-five days. In Fredericton only twenty-three. Tim Horton's is kind to give us work."

"The lady told me your mother is a very good cook."

"My mother was a cook in Hotel Four Seasons Damascus."

"Did you live in Damascus?"

"In small town outside."

There was so much I wanted to ask this girl. Even having watched news coverage for months, I had little understanding of what was really happening where she came from. I knew a bit of the geography of her country. I knew civil war had ravaged the cities. I knew her journey from some small town outside of Damascus to the capital city of New Brunswick was likely a long one, and that there'd probably not been anything easy about it. I wanted to know more but felt my prying and my ignorance would be an insult to her.

Amira opened the door of the garbage receptacle and pulled out the bag, tying it at the top.

"Can I help you?" I asked.

"Do you have a jacket? I take the bags out back."

"No. I left it behind. I was in a bit of a hurry."

"I know that way. Take mine, I have a sweater."

I took her offer and put her jacket on then grabbed one of

the bags, following her out the door.

Amira lifted the cover of the dumpster and threw her two bags in, then reached for mine.

"Did you sleep tonight?" she asked.

"No, not really."

"Come to my home. A short walk. You can sleep and I give you a jacket."

"That would be really nice of you."

"I will go tell Mother. She worries. She will be happy I have friend to walk with."

I walked back inside with Amira and waited as she called to her mother. Again, the embrace I was witnessing seemed emotional. Amira stroked her mother's head and spoke in a mix of English and, I assumed, Arabic.

"I will come back and get you. I will lock the door. I will be fine."

As we walked out the door, I could see Amira wiping a tear from her eye.

"She is so afraid. I am all she has left, and when we part she worries. She is better but still so afraid."

I thought about my mom and the fear I saw in her eyes every day. Not to dismiss my mother's loss, but I imagined that the horrors Amira and her mother had lived were much greater than ours. Could losses be compared, rated, and evaluated—and if they could, would that help the healing or the acceptance? I remembered words of comfort that were offered after Mike's death. One lady had said repeatedly that at least Mom still had two other children. She had referred to a recent accident in Moncton that killed all three children in a family. The comment had made Mom angry.

Could pain and loss be itemized and processed in this way? I was anxious to know about Amira's journey, but would learning about it help to put my own in perspective? Is that how things worked? Finding a grief scale and finding where you fit on it and going on from there?

We walked along the street, not saying a word to one another. I thought of Amira and her mother's good-bye and compared it to how distant Mom and I were from each other these days. I remembered her being sound asleep when I left the house yesterday morning and all the other nights I came home or stayed away and she hadn't even noticed. Had her worry and anxiety that something more might happen caused behaviour all the way on the other end of the spectrum from that of Amira's mother, who had such difficulty letting her daughter out of her sight? Both ways showed pain and despair; was one any better than the other?

"Is it just your mother and you left?"

"Yes. I had three brothers, two older and one younger. And my father, of course. My mother saved us by leaving, but her braveness was in vain. War kills in many ways, but I refuse to let it have my mother. I am now the one that must stay strong."

"How old are you?"

"Eighteen. My mother was already married with a child by the time she was my age. I dream of being a doctor and maybe Canada will give me that. I cared for the sick in the camp and many say I have the gift."

"Did you live in a refugee camp?"

"Yes, in Lebanon."

I thought of how difficult it sometimes was to tell strangers about Mike's accident. I did not expect this girl to blurt out all the details of the losses and devastation that was her story. She would tell me what she wanted, when she wanted.

"You must think Canada very cold."

"There was snow when we came and I had not seen that much snow before. We have cold, but not like yours."

We turned a corner and came to a large red brick building. Amira led me to the side and we began walking up a steep set of enclosed stairs.

"Mrs. Mary found us this lovely home. Mother cries when

the taps bring water."

Amira took a key from a chain around her neck and un-locked the door. The *lovely* home seemed small and cramped. The open room served as kitchen, living room, and bedroom, and it wasn't much bigger than our family room. The blankets on the pullout couch were pulled up neatly. Amira lifted a pillow and took a folded blanket from off the armchair, pointing to the couch.

"You can lie there and sleep. I will make meal for you to eat when you wake."

Probably it was rude to accept her offer so quickly, but as I stood looking at the couch, I realized just how tired and completely overwhelmed I was. A few hours of sleep would be a welcome escape, so, saying nothing, I simply kicked off my sneakers and lay down. Amira covered me with the blanket and turned off the overhead light and I settled into a relieved, grateful, and secure relaxation.

# CHAPTER 13

The sun was streaming through the window when I woke up. I'd slept so soundly I hadn't heard Amira in the kitchen directly behind me, but I smelled something amazing. I sat up and turned around to see her standing in front of the small stove. Everything in the kitchen seemed miniature. Even the refrigerator was the size of Dad's beer fridge in the basement.

"You are awake. You will want the bathroom." She pointed to the door on the end wall. "Have shower if you like. I get towels for you."

"Thank you. It is so kind of you to have me in your home. I really appreciate it."

"Many people kind to us. It is nothing."

"I think it's a lot. You don't even know me."

"I know you are alone. You are frightened?"

"I was. I didn't know what I was going to do. I still don't, but your kindness will help me figure it out."

"Did someone hurt you?"

"Almost. I got away. That is why I have no jacket and I don't have my phone and my things."

Amira flinched. "We left in the night. Mother woke us and we took all we could carry. I left many things behind. Mother carried my small brother, and Houda, my oldest brother, walked on crutches. We carried very little. I know the sorrow."

"No, no, I'm fine. My friends will probably bring me my bag. I just don't want to see them today."

"Shower and I finish the falafel."

It was a small enclosed shower stall with just a trickle of water, but the heat felt wonderful. I leaned into the stream and let it soak my hair. My body began shaking and tears came in a flood almost stronger than the shower's water pressure. I could have been recovering this morning from an assault. If that encounter in the cramped tent had been what Ethan Rogers anticipated, I would have been changed forever. I would have the terrible memory of that act being my first sexual encounter, along with the possibility of a pregnancy.

Somehow, I'd gotten away, even if I'd been dumb enough to fall for the fake kindness. Ethan's mean words and my brother's wisdom saved me.

"I love you, big brother." I spoke those words out loud and let the crying come.

I towel-dried my hair and got dressed. As I walked out into the main room, I could see the table was set and Amira was setting a plate of food down.

"I hope you will like. It is falafel in pita with lettuce, tomatoes, and tahini."

"If it tastes even half as good as it smells, it will be wonderful."

I sat down and picked up the warm pita. The first bite proved my prediction to be correct. The combination of spices, sauce, and tomato was delicious, along with the crunchy balls and crisp lettuce. It was like nothing I had tasted before.

"This is really good. What did you call it?"

"Falafel. I make ball from ground chickpeas and spices, then deep fry. The tahini is made with sesame seeds and olive oil. We eat it on many things."

"Well, it is delicious," I said, taking another bite.

"And filling, it will stay with you."

When I'd finished, I cleared the table as Amira filled the dishpan with hot soapy water.

"Mother still cannot believe we turn a tap and hot water comes. While we walked we took small mouthfuls and prayed for water along the way. Sometimes days would go by with just one bottle for us all. For so many months even getting enough water to wash with was almost impossible. And such dirty water once we came to Bekaa. It was the dirty water that made Bushra die. He was too weak to fight the bad water germs."

"That is so sad. I'm so sorry."

"Mother gets angry sometimes. She sees good water wasted and good food. She cries some days when she returns from work. People leaving good food on their plates for the garbage when she has seen so many go hungry."

"What was your life like before the war?"

"Father was a farmer. He grew large fields of tobacco on land his father owned before him. He built us a comfortable house. Mother travelled by bus to Damascus to cook. Many cousins and aunts and uncles lived nearby until the bombing started."

There were a couple of minutes of silence before Amira asked, "What is your sadness?"

"How do you know I am sad?"

"I saw it in your eyes when we first talked. I have learned that most people have their own sadness."

"My brother Mike died a year ago. He was in a bus accident."

"I am sorry. I know the sadness. My brother Omran was my first loss. I thought my heart would break."

"How old was he?"

"He was twenty—just a boy, really, but he thought he was a man. He was so hopeful for a better Syria. Hopeful and foolish, I know now. The troops had no respect for his dreams."

I could hardly grasp what she was telling me. I knew from the news that Syrian troops killed thousands of their own people. I would not ask her for the exact details.

"After Omran was killed, Mother begged Father to leave as thousands around us were doing, but he would not listen."

"You said your other brother was on crutches. Was he injured?"

"No. Houda was born with twisted leg. He did not walk for many years and then walked with a crutch."

I waited. Again, I would not pressure Amira for the details of her losses. I could not even imagine taking what I felt in losing Mike and multiplying it.

"We are in Canada because of my brother's crippled leg. The authorities saw a widow with a crippled son and showed mercy. Our asylum was granted because of Houda. He was our saviour and our life today we thank him for."

Amira got up from the chair and went to the cupboard. "I will make you tea and give you some of Mother's baklava. You will like."

The kettle boiled, the tea was made, and a square of pastry set in front of me before Amira spoke again.

"Sweet Houda. He died in a battle but not with others. The battle he lost was with himself."

I took a sip of the hot, sweet tea. Amira's tears streamed down her cheeks and I could clearly see the pain of this loss was very deep.

"We were to leave the next day. All arrangements had been made and Mother was overjoyed. She was of course frightened about what was ahead, but the thought of a life without war and hunger was enough to fill her with hope. She buried a husband and two children and believed her sorrows were ending. I felt a troubling feeling watching Houda that night as many gathered to celebrate our leaving. He was so quiet."

Amira walked across the room to get a tissue and wiped her tears.

"After the celebration, Houda climbed to the highest hill nearby. From there he could see Syria. He hanged himself from the branches of a tall cedar. The note he left told of his shame in not being able to fight beside his brother and father for his beloved homeland. He said a man that runs from battle is a coward and he would stay."

I reached out and put my arms around Amira's shoulders. She allowed herself to rest her head against me while her tears turned to sobbing.

"Houda was no coward," she said after her sobbing quieted.

"I think you have all been so brave. You and your mother have come to a strange country to make a new life and it must not be easy. I feel my family has been cowardly and our situation has been nothing compared to what you've had to face."

"I do not wear my story like a badge. Many people have suffered much loss. My father did not die alone."

"Does thinking of it that way make your sorrow easier to bear?"

"No, not easier. But it gives me strength and courage. It also makes me determined to live the life my father dreamed of for me. I cannot change the past, only move toward a brighter future."

Amira got up and poured herself a cup of tea. She sat across from me and took a sip before speaking. "There is no measuring pain. When we lose those we love, we must walk our own path to healing."

"You can truly say that. You *did* walk to find a better life. You walked and hoped. My family is just stuck in our pain. My mother stays in her bed. My father and sister are travelling all over the country. They think they're chasing my sister's dream, but I think they're running away from the sadness. I have been so angry and so lonely."

"I was very angry with Houda at first. I could not forgive him for the pain he caused my mother. I fought the anger to find the peace I needed to help her survive."

"I left home to come to a concert. I came to hear my brother's favourite band. I came for that, but mostly I was trying to force my mother to miss me. I want her to choose another way of living without Mike. It seems pretty stupid after hearing your story."

"It is not stupid. You must deal with what you are given. It is not for us to choose."

"How far did you walk?"

"We walked for three weeks. I do not know how far. Many people pay money for bus fare, for car rides, or for promise of a place on the back of trucks. Often money is paid then no transport available. Walking is dangerous but not as costly." She smiled sadly.

I looked across the table at this girl not much older than me who had been through so much. I was fewer than two hundred kilometres away from home. I had no bus ticket and only a few dollars, but I wasn't facing any of the dangers that Amira had survived.

"If it is money you need to get home, I have some I can give you. I know you do not want to travel on the bus with the man who hurt you, but you could take another bus at a different time. You can stay here as long as you need to. Mother will not mind."

"Thank you. I haven't figured out what I should do. If I called my neighbour or my aunt, I know they would come for me. I'm embarrassed to do that, though. I wanted to make this trip on my own and prove I wasn't weak, I guess."

"Do not think yourself weak. You have not suffered war and the suffering it brings, but your pain has been real and you have done your best. You will figure it out. You must do what you feel. I can give you a backpack and some food and water to take on the bus if you need. I must go for Mother soon. You can stay until I return or leave with me. You can always come back if you need to."

"Thank you so much, Amira. I appreciate your kindness. I will leave with you when you go for your mother and figure out a plan."

I looked over to the small table beside the couch, where I could see a cordless phone.

"I was wondering if I might use your phone to call my neighbour just to tell her I'm okay. I am afraid that when I don't get home tonight, my family will be very worried."

"Of course. I told Mrs. Mary we did not need a telephone. We have no one to call, but she said that that will change once we get to know more people. I now have you to call! A real friend in Canada."

I took the corner of the napkin from my jeans pocket and dialled Alice's number.

"Hello, Alice. It's Franny. I'm at a friend's house in Fredericton."

"Oh, I am glad you called, dear. Are you all right?"

"Yes, I'm fine. I was wondering if you could go over and tell my mother I called. I lost my phone."

"Oh dear. Well, of course I can. Lesley came yesterday."

"Did my uncle and the kids come with her?"

"Yes, they did. Those two kids have sure grown. Are you all right, Franny? Lesley said you went to a concert?"

"Yeah. I'm fine. Can you tell them I'll be home in a couple of days? I've had to change my plans a bit."

"Do you have a way home? I can come get you."

"No, it's fine. Just tell them not to worry. Thanks so much, Alice. Good-bye."

I hung up quickly, not giving Alice a chance to ask me anything more. I'd decided what my way home was. I was going to walk.

I sat on the couch and considered the reality of that plan. I would not tell Amira my whole plan or my reasoning for it. Walking all the way home was how I could show courage and make this trip count for something. I would just tell Amira that I was walking to Oromocto to borrow bus fare from Alice's sister, stay the night there, and catch the bus tomorrow. My walk home would not hold any of the perils her family faced on their journey, and I would not insult her by pretending it did.

"My neighbour suggested I go to her sister's in Oromocto and stay the night. She will give me bus fare and I'll catch the bus there tomorrow."

Amira brought over a backpack and set it on the couch beside me.

"How far is this walk?"

"I don't know. Not too far. It might take me a couple of hours."

"Are your shoes comfortable?" Amira pulled the top drawer of a dresser open and took out socks. "I will pack some Band-Aids. The blisters may come and you will need to keep your socks dry. I will give you two pairs. I will give you a sweater and a blanket just in case."

"My sneakers will be fine. Just a jacket would be great."

"Having more, better than not. I am giving you this new package of underwear."

"I don't need them, Amira."

"So much kindness has been shown to us. I can do the same. Toilet paper," she added as she hurried into the bathroom.

A few minutes later, Amira placed the food she'd prepared on top of everything else in the backpack and we were ready to leave the apartment.

"Do you have *any* money?" Amira asked.

"Yes, I have about ten dollars."

"I give you ten more."

"I'm fine. You have given me food and water. I shouldn't need to buy anything more."

"Take ten more. You can repay me. We are friends, more like sisters, and we will see each other again."

We didn't talk as we walked along the street. There were about seven hours of daylight left. By dark, I wanted to be far enough along the highway to find a sheltered place to sleep for the night.

I was afraid but also excited about what I was undertaking. At least the others had already left Fredericton, so there would be no chance of the bus passing me and them seeing me walking. I was walking a different way, anyway. I was going to walk along the river, past the Fredericton airport, and then on to Oromocto. I wasn't completely sure of the way, but I remembered picking Aunt Lesley up at the Fredericton airport a couple of years ago, driving into Fredericton and then back home that way.

There would be signs and I could ask for directions along the way. I would know the way for sure once I got to the familiar highway between Oromocto and Westfield. I could take the Westfield ferry and walk across the peninsula to the Gondola Point ferry and into Quispamsis. I knew the peninsula fairly well from our summers renting a cottage there and from visiting Tara's grandmother in Bayswater. Thinking about my route and mapping it out in my head was probably a lot easier than actually walking it was going to be.

I hugged Amira, not anxious to let go and head out alone.

"I will pray," Amira said. "I will pray for your mother and your family."

"And I will keep you and your mother in my thoughts and prayers."

I began walking, not looking back, afraid that if I did I would rush back to her side and change my plan. I picked up my pace, determined to walk the first few blocks quickly so that turning back would become less likely. If I was going to gain courage, I had to begin the quest for it. I thought of Amira and her mother and brothers heading out along familiar roads until they'd reached the point where they knew for sure they had truly left. I was heading toward the familiar by finding my way through the unknown.

I got all the way to the airport before I stopped. I entered the building knowing a washroom awaited me there. I would wash my face and take a bit of a rest, eat one of the pitas and some fruit Amira had packed for me. It was almost six. There were three more hours of light, but did I have three more hours of energy?

It hadn't been too bad, so far. There'd been lots to look at, lots of traffic. Kids rode by on bikes and several people spoke to me, making the four hours go by quickly. Probably on the highway the walking would seem more solitary, with vehicles just flying by me. Certainly, sleeping under the stars would provide thinking time, too.

The weather was warm and the sky a clear, deep blue. No clouds meant no rain, and for that I was thankful. Parts of the walk took me along the banks of the Saint John River. That same river was the one at the cottage our family rented several summers on the Kingston peninsula. My memories of the weeks spent there were some of my best. I had learned to swim in the shallow water at Ernie Gorham's camp. It had been at least three years since Dad made arrangements to rent it. It wasn't even a consideration last summer. The summer before, Mike had a summer job at Sobeys so Mom wouldn't go. Maybe this year we could rent it again. Mike carved his name in the rafters the first year and I would love to go and see that.

I used the washroom. I slipped off my sneakers and socks, rubbing my right heel. No blister, just a red mark. I noticed a box of garbage bags on the shelf above the sink. I pulled two out and crammed them in my backpack. The ground could be damp to lie on. I retied my sneakers. I was a bit stiff, but I was okay.

It was six-thirty when I walked out of the airport. I would walk until at least eight-thirty, stopping while it was still light enough to choose a spot to sleep for the night.

Aunt Lesley and Uncle Craig were at my house. I was looking forward to seeing Jordan and Riley. It would be great to have a four- and a six-year-old in the house for a while. Kids that age couldn't be ignored.

I hadn't asked Alice if Dad and Jenny had come home. I

wondered if Mom or Aunt Lesley had even called them. It wasn't as if me going to a concert was an emergency. But maybe Aunt Lesley would understand that everything I wrote about Mom was enough to warrant bringing Dad and Jenny home. They were part of the problem; they needed to be part of the solution.

The solution. What exactly was that? Nothing we could do would bring Mike back. I thought of Amira, her mother, and her two brothers leaving their home and walking, knowing they were leaving her father and oldest brother in graveyards. I assume they were buried, but I didn't know that for sure. We at least were given a body and could bury Mike in a peaceful place. There had been so much war, so much destruction in Amira's country that probably even hospitals, churches, and graveyards had been bombed.

And I wasn't sure what her traditions even were. Her mother and she wore headscarves, so I figured they were Muslim, but I didn't know anything about Islam, really.

Mike had had a church funeral, even though we never went to church. The minister was really nice, but Dad asked that there be no sermon. He wasn't interested in Mike's death becoming a selling point for salvation. The church people had been very kind. The funeral was huge, and they set up a sound system in the basement so that everyone could hear the service.

I remembered walking Mom through the crowd so that she could use the bathroom before the service started. She was in a daze. She stood up and gave Mike's eulogy, though. I didn't know how she did that. I had spoken, too, but just to say a few words about the song I'd chosen to be played while the casket was taken from the church. I figured if Mom could find the courage to speak, I could, too.

It was the theme song for *The Dukes of Hazzard*. In our old house, Mike and I had shared a room. We were just little, but I always remembered the poster on the wall of the Duke boys, Daisy Duke, and the General Lee. Mike loved that show. I knew "Good Ol' Boys" was the right song.

Everyone had said how strong Mom and I were at the funeral. In some ways, the days right after were easier than all that followed. Strength was a funny thing, anyway. Some might see Miriam's dependence on her daughter as weakness and not see the strength it took for both of them to get to where they were.

It didn't matter what other people saw or thought. As a family, we needed to build each other up and find some new strength. I was looking forward to getting home and really trying to make sure we did that. I was not going to keep pretending we could all do it separately as we just got farther and farther from each other.

I heard the barking when I was still in the cover of the wooded stretch I took advantage of when I saw several houses on both sides of the road ahead. Amira was wise to pack toilet paper. I felt a bit guilty leaving my garbage on the ground, but knew it would decompose quickly—not like the plastic bags I could see littering the ditches. As I walked back out to the road, I could hear the barking getting louder; it was coming from behind the fence in front of the house I was walking by. I hoped the fence enclosed the whole yard.

"Disco!"

*Disco was a dark chapter in musical history.* Mike's dismissal of an entire music genre popped into my mind as the dog's owner stood on her front steps calling her barking dog.

"Disco!"

The woman opened the gate just as a huge black dog came around the end of the fence and bounded toward me.

"He won't hurt you."

As the beast got closer, I felt no confidence in the owner's words. I was going to be mauled to death with Gloria Gaynor singing "I Will Survive" in my head. How ironic was that?

"Disco. Come here!"

My killer stopped short in his tracks and then moved toward the woman, his tail wagging like crazy.

"He's a big baby, but he likes to pretend he's my guard dog. I'm sorry if he scared you. I normally keep him in the backyard if I'm not outside with him. He does like to run after the kids on bikes."

The woman brought the dog over to me, instructing him to sit, and I patted his big black head. He looked at me as if he were apologizing. His owner passed me a dog treat.

"Ask for his paw then give him his treat. I'm really sorry he scared you."

I patted Disco one more time and started walking again, tempted to break into song, the first two lines of Gloria Gaynor's song so fitting for what just happened. *First I was afraid, I was petrified...*

I laughed to myself, thinking if a movie was made of this walk the song, "I Will Survive," would play over the credits. The song was perfect for the last year, too. Maybe I should play it as soon as I got home and insist we all listen, maybe even disco dance to it. Maybe a theme song was what we needed to get our act together.

Who would I want to play me in the movie? Meryl Streep or maybe Susan Sarandon could play Mom. Although maybe they were too old. Maybe Julia Roberts or Nicole Kidman would be better. Taylor Swift could play Jenny. I wanted Ellen Page to play me. Strong, funny, and not easily flustered. I loved her character in *Juno*.

Thank God *I* wasn't worrying about whether I was pregnant or not.

The smoke of a nearby barbecue interrupted my train of thought. I was not hungry—but the smell had overtaken my senses. When was the last time Dad had barbecued? I couldn't remember him barbecuing at all last summer, even though most summers he fired up the barbecue almost every night, taking great pride in his grilling skills.

I could hear the family noises coming from behind the house where I could now pinpoint where the scent of barbecuing was coming from. I stopped a moment to take in the sounds. Kids, a mother, a dad, a small dog yapping. I started walking again.

The dad would be played by Mark Wahlberg, and not just because he looked so good without a shirt. I shouldn't care about that. It was my dad, for God's sake. Zac Efron could play Mike. He would just have one scene at the beginning.

Would it show the bus accident?

I was getting tired and ridiculous. I didn't expect I was in for a good night's sleep on the ground, but maybe if I was able to fall asleep quickly, I could get up before daybreak and get a good start in the cool of the day. If I walked to a school, maybe the playground would have an enclosure of some kind that I could sleep in. If I got there just as it was getting dark, probably there wouldn't be any kids hanging out.

I'd been to an elementary school in Oromocto one time. Jenny had an exchange thing with the pen pals her grade five teacher had set up with the teacher there and Mom drove. I'd gone along, too. I remembered it was quite close to the high school. I played soccer at the high school several times. If I got on the right road, I could find my way there.

Wassis Road. I saw the sign a little way ahead of me. It was almost eight-thirty now. I wondered how long it would take me to walk to the elementary school. I would just have to see. It would be fine if it was dark when I got there. I would just make sure no one was around and camp in the small enclosure I remembered seeing on the platform above the slide.

I was getting quite eager for my first day of walking to end. You would think I was heading to a Best Western and a big bed heaped with pillows instead of a dirty wooden platform with a lifetime supply of discarded gum stuck to its undersurface.

# CHAPTER 14

It was just about dark when I got to Assiniboine Elementary School. I was relieved to find no one there, not even in the yards of the surrounding houses. I imagined if someone saw a girl bedding down on the playground, they might call the police. I wanted to get right to sleep and wake myself up before daybreak. I certainly didn't want curious kids waking me up.

I was really tired. With the turmoil of the night before and the walking I had done since leaving Amira, I felt exhausted. It was a warm night, and hopefully the blanket Amira packed for me would be enough. I would leave my clothes on, too, of course. I wanted to be ready to move if something or someone should wake me.

I took the food from the backpack and wrapped it in my jacket. I hoped that it wouldn't attract an animal. I shoved it in the corner of the playground enclosure that was my accommodation for the night. I laid out the garbage bags on the wooden platform and plumped up my backpack for my pillow, lay down, and covered myself with the fleece blanket.

The night sounds were soothing, and I felt myself relaxing. I wouldn't have thought I would find myself sleeping outside, but I was determined to not let my imagination run away with me. My sleeping arrangements tonight did not hold the threat of last night's, when I had naively curled up in Ethan's tent expecting it to be a safe haven.

I awoke with a jolt to a sound that seemed to be right beside my head. When I sat up, though, I could tell it was coming from across the playground next to the school. An animal had gotten into the garbage barrel and was struggling to get itself out. The barrel was teetering, then a couple of seconds later it fell on its side and a huge raccoon staggered away as if it were getting off a carnival ride.

The sun was just beginning to come up in the distance. I had actually slept all night. I stood up and stretched a bit, then got down off the platform and squatted beside the slide to pee. Getting back onto the platform, I unwrapped the food and put my jacket on. I folded up the garbage bags and the blanket and stuffed them in my backpack, then set the food in on top. I would get started on my way.

I began walking toward where I remembered there being a Tim Horton's. There were two in Oromocto, but if I went to the farther one I would be closer to the highway when I finished washing up and eating. I was anxious to brush my teeth, wash my face with hot water, and have coffee.

I could see lights coming on in houses along the street. There was something magical about this time of the morning—not that I saw it very often. I had forgotten that today was a holiday Monday. The playground wouldn't have filled with kids in a couple of hours and I probably could have slept longer, but I was glad I was up. I probably wouldn't have gotten back to sleep anyway. I was lucky to have slept soundly for so long.

Once I started walking along the highway, there wouldn't be anywhere to stop. I decided to keep the food Amira packed for later and buy something to eat at Tim Horton's. I'd buy more water, too, as it could be a hot day by the feel of the temperature already.

I entered the lockable family restroom. It was good to be able to wash and change my underwear with no chance of someone walking in on me. I felt refreshed as I walked out.

"Franny Callaghan. What a surprise!"

Coming through the main door was my neighbor, Sue McEachern.

"Hi, Mrs. McEachern. What are you doing here?"

"I've been visiting a friend in Burton. I hate that Broad Road after dark so I decided to stay last night and get an early start this morning. I didn't even wake her, just got on my way. I'm stopping for a coffee and a bite to eat. What brings *you* here so bright and early?"

"I'm visiting a friend, too. Same thing, didn't want to wake her so I walked here for breakfast. I love their maple French toast bagels. Have you tried them?"

"No. Maybe I'll get myself one. Go sit down and I'll order. What else would you like? My treat."

While Mrs. McEachern was placing the order, I considered whether or not I should ask her for a drive home. If I left with her, I would be home just as everyone at my house was getting up. I was tired from the walking I did yesterday and I knew I had a long walk ahead of me. I was sure if Amira and her family had had the opportunity to get a drive to Lebanon with a friendly neighbour, they would have taken the offer.

Mrs. McEachern brought the tray over and sat down. "This bagel looks delicious. So glad you told me about them. I usually just get a breakfast sandwich."

I took a bite of my bagel and a drink of coffee. I was a bit reluctant to begin small talk, afraid to get my lies mixed up. I had told her I was visiting a friend. I let silence fill the next few moments while both of us drank our coffee and ate.

"Alice came over a week ago. She told me your mom has not been doing well. I'm so sorry, Franny. I stopped going over months ago and I shouldn't have. I can't even imagine what she's going through. I took some cookies over yesterday. Your aunt and uncle and cousins are visiting, eh? That's nice."

"Yes. I haven't seen them yet. I left for my friend's house before they got there. They surprised Mom."

"I saw the memorial in the paper. Hard to believe it's been a year."

"I know."

"How are you doing, Franny? I'm sure it's been really hard on you, especially with your mom not doing well."

"It's been hard, but we're all doing the best we can."

"The nice weather might help. Your mom does love her garden."

I didn't answer. What good would it do to tell Mrs. McEachern that Mom couldn't care less about her garden or anything else these days? I imagined myself getting a drive home with her and getting dropped off. I wasn't ready to face the disappointment if the changes we so desperately needed at my house weren't happening.

I had to keep walking so that I could find the strength to believe in healing for my family. If I took the easy way out now, I would only have myself to blame if nothing changed.

"Thanks so much for breakfast. When you get home, would you mind going over and telling Mom you saw me? Tell her I'll be home by Wednesday, Thursday at the latest. I misplaced my phone, so I haven't been able to text her."

"Haven't you called her from your friend's house?"

Damn. I was not thinking things through clearly enough to lie well. "Yeah, of course. But you know what moms are like. She'll be happy to know you saw me."

"Don't you have to be home for school tomorrow? You're still in school, aren't you?"

"Yeah. Grade eleven. It's kind of a school exchange thing I'm on here."

I felt terrible lying to her, especially since she would probably know I was lying as soon as she went over to tell Mom my message. I would have to apologize and explain later, but if I told her the truth now, I was sure she would not be leaving Oromocto without me.

I waited until she drove out of the parking lot before going to the counter to buy three bottles of water. The drive-through line was right out to the road and a steady stream of camo-wearing soldiers were coming in and out of the building. I glanced at the clock on the wall: 7:40. I picked up my backpack and walked out the door.

I'd told Sue McEachern Wednesday or Thursday. I wasn't sure how far I would get today, but knew I would be sleeping somewhere along the highway tonight and sleeping outside somewhere tomorrow night as well. I actually had no idea how long it was going to take me to walk all the way home. At least by saying Thursday, it might help Mom manage her worry. It felt good, actually, that she might be worrying, but I didn't want to torture her. At least knowing that Sue had seen me would help.

I walked along the ramp leading to the highway. Which side of the road should I be walking on when I hit the busy highway? I didn't want anyone thinking I was hitchhiking, so I decided to walk facing traffic. I would have to cross the four lanes of the busy highway, and the morning traffic was quite steady. I did not let my mind wander until I had safely gotten on the other side. Then I walked as far over on the shoulder as I could without going in the ditch.

The first diversion I created was a red-car count. I had to get to one hundred before letting myself sit down for a break and an apple. I developed a steady pace and kept focused on the car count. Red was definitely one of the most common car colours. I was glad I hadn't committed to counting blue ones, or it might have been hours before I could take a break. There were several shades of red, but anything from burgundy to a fire-engine red qualified.

I reached one hundred before I came to a good place to sit and rest, so I was more than ready to sit when I finally did. As I took a bite of my apple, I wondered if I had used the car counting as a way to keep me from having to think about my purpose and the point of walking. I didn't want to second-guess my decision not to take a drive from Mrs. McEachern. All my philosophical reasons for walking were harder to embrace when I was actually walking and could not see an end in sight. It was a long way home.

I needed to focus and not let the magnitude of the journey get to me. One step at a time. Just put one foot in front of the other. Don't bite off more than you can chew. The quote from *The Fellowship of the Ring* came to mind: Not all those who wander are lost.

I was perfectly fine. My feet didn't hurt yet. I had food and water. I was walking safely and the chances of getting hit by a car were slim. I would just keep going. Nothing ventured, nothing gained. You don't win a game of chess unless you make a move. My mind was a jumble of quotes and clichés. I needed to get it together or they might find me wandering weeks from now mumbling lines from movies and songs.

I thought back to the concert and the feeling I had had listening to the songs Mike had listened to over and over. The road we take can lead us home. I wished I had my iPod or my phone and could listen to the song for real. Familiar music would have motivated me.

Was that true, or was I just afraid to be alone with no distractions and really listen to my own thoughts? Maybe that was the most important part of this walk. I only had myself to rely on. I had no technology, nothing to use as an excuse for not paying attention. This long, lonely trip was forcing me to be entirely with myself.

It seemed to me that being with herself was not working for Mom. She was hiding. She had given up. How could days and months of retreating to your room be a good thing? And was my aloneness on this walk any different? There was risk, at least. I was fairly confident I was in no real danger, but I was still vulnerable in some ways.

My thoughts were interrupted by a shadow that made me

turn my head. Above me, close enough that I could see the white head and a small animal hanging from its talons, was a bald eagle. It swopped in a dancelike motion and I was mesmerized. Besides the fear that it might drop its dinner on my head, I was in awe of its beauty.

Nature. On both sides of the highway, thick stands of trees provided the beauty of nature, and that was something Mom had been running from as well. She loved her gardens. She loved swimming, and last year she hadn't gone to her friend's beach once. She never went for walks anymore and hadn't gone snowshoeing on the trails at all last winter. I needed to convince Mom to get outside and enjoy nature again.

Falling asleep last night at the school, I'd heard dogs barking, traffic, people's voices, the wind. I hadn't been afraid of those sounds. I needed to help Mom see life in a way that didn't frighten her. There were scary things in this world, we knew that, but there were amazing things, too, and we sometimes had to put aside our fear to truly enjoy them. Somehow Mom had lost her courage.

I took the last bite of my apple and threw the core as far into the woods as I could. Maybe some squirrel or raccoon would come upon the tasty little treat. I stood up, trying to decide whether I had to retreat into the woods a bit farther to relieve myself before going on. No, I was fine for now. There would be lots of woods along the way.

I looked up at the sun, trying to guess the time. Dad always said that the sun was directly overhead at noon. I hadn't needed to use that knowledge before, as telling time simply meant looking at the screen of my phone. It didn't really matter what time it was, anyway. I would just keep walking until I stopped for a pee break or to eat something. I needed to be mindful of the amount of food I still had and just eat small amounts at a time. I could come off the highway in Welsford and go to the store, but that probably wouldn't be until tomorrow.

A while later, I was caught up in my thoughts, trying to remember something about the vacation we had all taken five years ago when we went to Canada's Wonderland. Mike and I had gone on every ride we could, some of them several times. The sound of air brakes interrupted me from trying to remember the name of the ride we got so wet on. I looked behind me and saw a huge transport truck backing up. I stepped into the ditch and up the side of the bank. The driver's door opened and a man stepped out and walked around the front of the truck to the shoulder of the road. Cars zipped by.

"What you doing out here by yourself, pretty girl?"

The man's tone and the look on his face made me uncomfortable. I stood my ground but considered just how quickly I could run if he came any closer. I could wave my arms and flag down a passing car. I could bolt across all four lanes to the other side of the road and run if I had to. He could come after me on foot, but he wouldn't be able to drive after me.

"My dad's picking me up soon."

"Your dad's pretty stupid to let you be walking all by yourself. Doesn't he know there's lots of perverts around?"

Takes one to know one. "He'll be here in a few minutes."

"A pretty girl like yourself. Someone might just come along and snatch you up. I could give you a ride to wherever you're headed. Wouldn't mind at all, sweet cheeks."

This guy was giving me the creeps. Even with a steady stream of cars going by, I felt that if he wanted to, he could reach across the ditch and haul me into his truck.

Staying on my side of the ditch, I started walking quickly. I tried to focus on the oncoming traffic while at the same time looking to see whether or not the guy was following me.

I heard him swear, then mutter, "Probably jailbait anyway."

I didn't turn around but kept walking, my heart pounding. I heard the truck door slam and looked to see the signal indicating he was pulling back out onto the road. This guy was very law-abiding. He followed the traffic laws and was not willing to violate a minor for fear of being jailed as a pedophile. For once I was thankful for my size and the fact that I looked younger than I was, instead of older.

I made a note of the company name on the side of the truck that the sleaze was driving, knowing perfectly well I wouldn't call and report him. What would I say? "Your driver stopped and offered me a ride."

Tears started running down my cheeks. I felt the terror of how badly that could have gone. I had just been feeling that my walk home held little danger, but danger sometimes comes when you least expected it. Sneaks right up and grabs you.

I'd wondered so many times whether Mike had seen the danger coming. I liked to think he'd been asleep and hadn't feel the bus swerve out of control. I hoped that the end had come fast and he didn't suffer from the pain or the fear. But I would never know for sure.

The next few hours were uneventful. Timberwolf Falls was the ride at Canada's Wonderland. Mike had convinced us all to get on it. He had downplayed the getting-wet aspect, and at first it seemed like a lazy river kind of ride. It might have been, except for the fact that you splash into a pool of water when the ride hits the bottom. We were all soaked. It was fun, though.

The whole day had been fun. We almost didn't go. Mom thought it was too much money, but Dad used the "You only live once" argument, as well as "We might never get this close to Canada's Wonderland again, Marilyn." She gave in. We didn't get any pictures that day, but I could remember everything about it. Well, maybe not all the names of the rides, but the fun.

Mike wouldn't get to Canada's Wonderland again, but maybe we needed to go and spend the day having fun as a family the way we did that day. He would want us to, I knew that much.

I sat down at around four o'clock. I didn't know the time for sure, but it felt like it did after school. The air was a bit cooler, the hot sun of the afternoon lower. There were a few more clouds, but they didn't look like rain clouds. I was counting on another clear night, as sleeping outside in the rain would not be pleasant—especially with no clothes to change into. I did have the sweater Amira had packed for me, but my jeans were the only pants I had.

I ate a pita. Amira had filled this one with rice and falafel, tomatoes, and hummus. It was delicious. I ate another apple and one square of baklava. I felt full and nourished enough to continue walking till dusk.

Most of the cars going by all day seemed to have day lights on, but as the sun got lower, the lights of the oncoming traffic became more distinctive. I squinted my eyes a bit and watched the flickering lights coming toward me. It was odd to feel so alone in the midst of such roaring activity. People filled these vehicles that sped by me, but I had no interaction with them at all. What were their sorrows, their worries, their concerns? Amira said that everyone had sorrow, but I couldn't know the sorrows of the people who rushed by me and they could not know mine. We had to slow down to learn about each other's pain. We also had to be open about our own.

In such a short time, Amira and I had been able to show each other the pain we carried. I never let Bethany, Marin, or Sam see my sorrow. I had cut Tara off because I felt she couldn't understand my pain. Mom stayed in her room to keep from letting anyone see her sorrow. Why had it been so easy for Amira and me?

What if I flagged down one of the cars speeding by, and when the car stopped I asked the people to tell me what made them sad, what sorrow they carried? First of all, they would think I was insane. Possibly they would call 911, explaining a lunatic was stopping cars on Highway 7.

Amira had said she could see sorrow in my eyes. Amira looked, cared, and then reached out. Bethany didn't look. I don't think she even looked at her own pain. So much of what she did screamed pain and sadness, but she was very careful to mask it and make sure she let people know loud and clear she wanted them to keep their distance.

What if the people who stopped told me of their pain? Then what? What had Amira done with my sadness? She hadn't changed it; she wasn't able to take it away. But by her recognizing it, acknowledging it, a bond was formed between us. It helped on some level. It had given me courage and hope. Maybe Mom needed to be heard, and to hear other people tell of their pain, to get out from under the heavy weight of hers.

I mentally made a list, wishing I had a piece of paper and a pen. Maybe if I recited the list often enough, it would be still in my head when I got home.

"Taking risks. Nature. Family fun. Friends. Grief group."

I said the five things again and again, reciting them like a grocery list. These things all felt so important right now. Was I fooling myself, thinking that as I walked I would be given the wisdom I needed to help Mom, to help our whole family? Would this list keep the power I felt it held right now? Was any of this going to be helpful to Mom? I had to believe it was, or I would sit down on the side of this road and weep. I would not be able to find the stamina to keep going.

I had no choice, though, did I? I put myself here and I needed to keep going to get myself home. Sitting down and giving up was not an option.

"Taking risks. Nature. Family fun. Friends. Grief group." I was singing the list now as I picked up my pace, changing from opera to country, knowing Mike would have gotten quite a kick out of my musical range. Another half hour or so and I would bed down for the night. I was almost finished day two of walking home.

# CHAPTER 15

The most difficult part of last night's sleep was the tree roots. I had lain the garbage bags down on what seemed like a good sleeping spot, under the shelter of a large tree, but its roots made an uneven bed. It seemed that however I moved, I had a root sticking in my side or lower back. I'd made the best of it as it was dark by the time I settled down and I didn't want to search blindly for a better spot.

The stretch of the highway I was walking along was part of the Gagetown military base. Gates and No Trespassing signs closed off the roads into the training grounds. Fencing on both sides of the highway prevented access to the woods, but several spots along the way provided a cover of trees deep enough to block the sights and sounds of the busy highway. I'd lain down last night confident that any wild animal I should be afraid of would be on the other side of the fence. I had wrapped up my food in my jacket again and this time stuck it up in the highest branches I could reach of the tree I was sleeping under. I was almost asleep when it occurred to me I should have put it in another tree in case the robbing animal needed to walk over me to climb up for its stolen meal.

I woke up just before daybreak. It seemed I was in tune with nature's clock already. With no place handy to walk this morning to wash up and get coffee, I relieved myself in the woods and brushed my teeth, swishing only a small mouthful of water out of my last bottle. I wouldn't be able to get another until I got to Welsford, and I wasn't sure how long that would take.

I ate some nuts, a banana, and a piece of baklava. I put a Band-Aid on a tender spot on my left heel and pulled on clean socks. After I got my sneakers laced, I packed my backpack. It seemed cooler today, but still no rain. I was going to try hard to keep a good pace and get to the Westfield Ferry today. I wanted to get across it and a little way along the road before I camped out for the night. That way I could walk the rest of the way tomorrow and get home before dark.

I watched the sun come up about a half hour after I began walking. The sunrise was amazing. The colours of the sky were making me emotional. A year before was the first day of the funeral parlour. Those two days had been strange and exhausting. For hours on end, people filed through the door. The lineup at one point was all the way out to the road. Jenny and I had stood on the counter of the bathroom to look out the small basement window at the line forming around the outside of the building. It was so weird seeing neighbours, friends, and total strangers waiting to come in and walk by Mike's casket.

At first we had all lined up in a perfect row. I'd see people I knew at the back of the lineup, and it was so odd talking to strangers as the people I knew well got closer to the front of the line. After a while Jenny and I got out of line, sometimes sitting in the other room or hanging out with friends outside. It was like a big, sad party, with never-ending streams of people hugging me, rubbing my back, or patting my head.

So sorry for your loss. If I'd had a dollar for every time that line was spoken during those two days, I would have earned enough to pay for the funeral. Although I had no idea how much the funeral cost. I wasn't there when Mom and Dad chose the casket and made the arrangements. We waited back at the house. Jenny and I picked six of Mike's friends to be pallbearers to carry Mike out of the church.

That had been one of the hardest parts, watching his friends carrying his casket down the aisle. But even harder than that was the last night at the funeral parlour, when we had to close Mike's casket. Mom sobbed, holding on to Mike's hand, and Dad had to force her to let go. I had only touched him once when we arrived on the first day. He was so cold.

When the pallbearers had carried Mike's casket out of the church and out to the graveyard, we followed like zombies. Dad held Mom up as the casket was lowered into the ground. Then Mom just walked away. No one went after her. We all just stood there, people hugging us and patting our backs.

We were in the car, Jenny and I in the back seat almost buried by the flower arrangements from inside the church. Dad was quietly waiting in the driver's seat. We sat like that while Mom kept walking. None of us said anything, and finally Mom turned around, walked to us, and got into the passenger side of the car. We drove home in silence. Our house was filled with people. Maybe Mom had needed those few minutes alone to retrieve the strength to get through the next few hours.

I started counting posts of the moose fence that ran along the edge of the woods across the ditch. Every few posts there were strange-looking openings with metal teeth that looked like a whisk. Apparently, an animal could get back through this gate if they somehow got out through the mesh-like fence.

Mrs. McEachern had mentioned hating to drive on this road after dark. It was probably because of the many moose-related accidents there were along this stretch. After one of those serious accidents, a woman had petitioned for this fence to be installed. Mom had worked with the woman's sister and she talked about it when building the moose fence was on the news a lot. Lately it had been on the news again because the fence needed fixing and some parts replaced.

One time when Tara and I were visiting her grandmother on

the peninsula, I'd met a woman whose son-in-law had been paralyzed in a moose accident. He and his wife were driving home from Ontario for their summer vacation when they hit a moose. They survived, but the man was paralyzed from the neck down, just like Sadie Daniels from my brother's orchestra. She would never walk again, never have a normal life. It would have been awful if that had happened to Mike—but it would have been better to have him in a wheelchair than not to have him at all.

The dark shadow caught my eye first, and then I heard the noise. Suddenly, not five feet away from me but, thankfully, on the other side of the fence, stood a massive, scruffy, blackish-brownish moose. The sound was like a loud snuffing noise. I stood perfectly still while the huge animal bowed its head and rammed the fence. It straightened back up and took some backwards steps. I noticed two little ones behind the big moose. This must be the mother, and she was not too happy about me being so close to her babies. Her head was bobbing, her ears twitching, and she backed up some more before ramming the fence again.

I stood still, very relieved the fence between us was in good shape. I would let her figure out the fact that she couldn't get any closer to me and I wasn't able to get near her babies. I hoped she would then take them and head into the woods. Several cars slowed down, which wasn't helping to calm down this mama moose any. I started walking, keeping my eye on the moose and the stretch of fencing ahead of me.

Finally she turned around, made sounds as if she were informing the twins of her plans, then bounded off on her long legs into the woods. The little ones tottered after her. I breathed a big sigh of relief. I was very thankful I hadn't met her on my side of the fence.

About an hour later, I came to a stretch where the highway divided. In the distance, I saw something and wasn't sure what it was until I got closer. A mangled bike frame was mounted on a post. Flowers were spread around the base and a wreath hung on the bike. A plaque was inscribed with a man's name and date he died.

Someone had been killed on this bike at this place on the road. Somewhere this person had a family who mourned for him. This place had taken his life and changed his family's lives forever. Now on that sunny May morning, the only thing to show what had happened there was the mangled frame and front wheel of the bicycle he'd been riding.

I thought of the stretch of highway in Quebec. Was there anything on the side of the road to mark the accident that had taken place there a year ago? Were there any flowers, any crosses, or any mangled bus parts to pay tribute to the lives lost that night? Maybe someday I would travel there and put up a cross or lay a wreath.

Did the family of the man who'd lost his life right here come to this spot regularly to remember him? Did erecting this memorial to him help them with their grief? Did knowing other people would see it, that his accident would be remembered, help with the healing?

*You're not the only one with problems, Franny.*

I sat down a little way away from the bicycle. I wiped my tears and opened my backpack to get out the last pita. Was it disrespectful to have my lunch near the place someone died? When Dad was little, his family used to have Sunday picnics in the graveyard on the old road from Sussex. He told us that every time we drove by it. Riverbank Graveyard, it was called. I used to think it was gross to have a picnic in a graveyard. Mike disagreed.

"The people are dead, Franny," he told me. "Dead and buried. It's not like they care."

Before taking the Welsford exit, I sat down and put another Band-Aid on my heel and one on the side of my other foot. Amira had been right about the blisters. I wished I was closer to the ferry. It was probably going to be dark by the time I got to the ferry. I would probably sleep on the beach at the campground on the other side. Maybe there would be a shelter there or maybe even a trailer I could get into. I knew that would be breaking and entering, but I wouldn't steal or vandalize anything.

It felt strange going into the Irving at Welsford. I hadn't talked to another human being since Mrs. McEachern at Tim Horton's yesterday morning. The guy who tried to get me into his truck didn't count. It was good to actually talk to someone. I took my time choosing food and juice. Some small talk took place at the checkout counter.

"Do you know how many kilometres it is to the Westfield ferry?" I asked.

"About ten, I think?"

She may as well have told me a hundred. Thinking about walking another step now that I had stopped seemed impossible. I tried not to let my feelings show on my face. Even if I blurted out my despair and told this woman behind the counter how exhausted I was, how sore my feet were, how I had been walking since two o'clock Sunday afternoon all the way from Fredericton, what would she have been able to do? I supposed I could ask to use the phone on the wall behind her. I could call home and see who could come get me.

"Do you cook hotdogs on that?" I asked, pointing to a machine farther down the counter.

"Yes, we used to keep the steamer full of hotdogs, but since the highway bypassed us, we don't get the customers we used to. Now I only put some on if a customer asks for one. Who would want to eat a wiener that's been sitting there all day?"

"I'll take two, please."

"Sure. Have a seat over at the table and I'll bring them to you. You look worn out. Where you coming from? You by yourself?"

"Yeah. I've been walking a while. I still have to walk to the

Westfield ferry. I'm training for a marathon."

Lies were coming so easily to me these days. A marathon, all right; with what prize at the finish line?

"Do you want a milkshake with that? I can make a decent milkshake. It'll be on the house. You look like you could use some sugar for the last leg of your walk."

"Great. Thanks! Can I have a chocolate one, please?"

"Two hotdogs and a chocolate milkshake coming right up."

Marjorie sat with me while I ate and she chatted away about her husband and her kids. She had two boys, seven and twelve. Her husband was a mechanic and had a garage beside their house. She had worked at the Esso down the road where on Christmas Eve a few years ago a guy came in with a gun, took the employee hostage, then burned the place down after letting the guy go.

"Scared the crap out of the community, I can tell you that," Marjorie explained. "I had just left. It could have been me he took hostage. It was a while before Tim let me even think about going back to work. I got on here about six months after, when it was clear Esso wasn't rebuilding. This place used to be real busy, which I liked. Tim doesn't like me here alone when I close up. But I figure you can't let stuff like that keep you from living. Things happen and there's nothing you can do about it."

I was considering opening up and telling Marjorie about Mike and about Mom. But she got up from the table to take money from the guy who was paying for his gas.

"Chuck's going right to the Westfield ferry," she called out after she rang in the sale. "I can vouch for the guy. He could give you a ride if you want one."

I considered the offer. If I took a ride, I'd get there before dark and could walk for a little while once I got across the ferry. Taking a short ride wouldn't hurt anything. I'd still be walking home.

"No, that's okay," I answered. "Got to get in my training."

The walk along the river gave me a lot to look at but wasn't enough to distract me from my sore feet and aching body. It was a really nice evening, and people were out in their yards. About every second house seemed to have someone pushing or riding on a lawn mower. I could smell freshly mown grass.

Dusk-to-dawn lights were starting to come on as I trudged along. I was really getting tired and hoped each bend I came to would be the one where I'd see the store directly across from the ferry landing. I crossed where the bridge led out to my mom's friend Alexandra and her husband's summer cottage. I knew the ferry was just a bit farther from there. I would walk by the RCMP station, a church, and a few more houses. The railroad tracks ran along the sidewalk I was now walking on. I started counting telephone poles. I walked quickly from pole to pole in anticipation of finally getting to my destination.

The ferry was just pulling in as I walked along the landing road. It was almost dark. I could see several cars waiting in line. As I walked by the row of cars I heard my name.

"Franny Callaghan, is that you?"

The voice sounded familiar, but I couldn't place it. Who was getting on this ferry that knew me?

"Franny, it's Nancy, Tara's grandmother. Come around and get in. It's cool out there."

I walked behind the car and opened the passenger door. I slid into the seat feeling relief at the warmth and the chance to sit down.

Nancy Doherty was Tara's grandmother, her dad's mother. Tara and I had spent many enjoyable visits at her house beside the Bayswater Bridge. For years, I considered this woman my own grandmother. I hadn't seen her since Tara and I had had our falling out. I felt overwhelmed as I sat in her car, realizing how much I had missed her and also feeling embarrassed by the fact her granddaughter and I weren't friends anymore.

"What are you doing walking onto the Westfield ferry all by yourself?"

I thought quickly, trying to come up with a believable lie, but instead blurted out the truth. "I walked here from Fredericton."

"You what?"

"Not all in one day, of course. I started walking Sunday afternoon. It's a long story."

"Well, you may as well tell me. First of all, does your mother know where you are?"

"Not really." Before I could say another thing, I started to cry. I was shaking and crying and completely out of control. My truthfulness had broken the dam I had carefully plugged with lies over the last few days.

Nancy reached over and put her hand on my shoulder. "You just let it out, sweetie. I don't know where you planned on sleeping tonight, but you're coming to my house. The first thing I'm going to do when we get there is call your mother and tell her where you are. You don't have to talk to her if you don't want to. You can take your time and tell me all about whatever it was that prompted you to walk from Fredericton—and why you were there by yourself in the first place. By the looks of it, you are overdue for a good long talk, and I'm just the old lady for the job."

I kept crying. Nancy drove off the ferry, and I looked through my tear-filled eyes at the campground where I thought I'd be sleeping tonight. I felt so relieved that Nancy had been getting on the ferry at the same time as me. My blisters were killing me, my legs were tired. I was sore, exhausted, and cold. The walk from Welsford had been harder and more miserable than all the rest. I'd cursed the fact I hadn't taken the drive I'd been offered over and over with every painful step. But now I was so glad I hadn't taken the drive with Chuck. If I had, I wouldn't have been here when Nancy was. I pressed my eyes closed.

*Thank you, Mike.*

# CHAPTER 16

Nancy's house was on a hill looking down at the Bayswater covered bridge. The steep hill in front was the best for sliding, and Tara and I would spend hours on cardboard boxes zooming down it right to the ditch by the road. In the summer, we swam from the shore on the other side of the bridge. The bigger kids jumped off the bridge, but we had never gotten up the nerve for that. The woods behind the house had a really nice trail that we used to play on, imagining we were all kinds of characters.

One day we'd found an old rock foundation in the field over from the house and explored all around it before actually climbing down in it. We got in big trouble. Her grandmother hollered at us and told us to stay away from there as it was dangerous and could collapse on us. She was really mad, and while she was hollering, telling us all the reasons we shouldn't go near it, tears were streaming down her cheeks. Then she made us fudge.

Nancy made the very best fudge and chocolate chip cookies. Blueberry cake, too. Tara and I used to pick blueberries for her. That's what we were doing when we found the old foundation. She made us blueberry pancakes that day after she'd finished hollering at us. Everything she cooked was delicious and she always spoiled us whenever we came to visit. She always sent treats home, too.

We pulled into Nancy's yard and Buddy ran over to the car, barking. Buddy was really old and I was so happy to see he was still living. I hadn't been here since Mike died. Nancy had come to the funeral parlour and the funeral. She had come back to the house afterwards, too. I'm sure she brought food with her that day, but I don't remember.

"I'm home, old boy," Nancy said, getting out of the car and patting Buddy. "Everything good on the home front? Look who I brought with me."

Buddy bounded around to my side. He used to jump up, but wagging his tail was the best he could do now.

"Hi, Buddy. You still know me?"

"Oh, he still knows you. He remembers all the people he loves. Remembers the ones he hates, too. He won't even let that young Seeley boy in the yard. Don't know what happened there, but Buddy holds a grudge."

"Tara and I aren't really hanging out together these days. Did she tell you we aren't friends anymore?"

Nancy looked at me kindly. "No, but she did say she doesn't see you much. Friendships run hot and cold sometimes."

"She didn't tell you what happened?"

"No, not really. You can tell me later if you want to. And either way, you're always welcome here, you know."

"Thank you." I followed Nancy into the familiar house.

Nancy set a bowl of Irish stew in front of me, then placed a plate of biscuits in the middle of the table. It felt so good to be in this familiar house being waited on and welcomed. I wanted to let the attention, the smell of the stew, and the warmth of the room take me back to the little girl I remembered being sitting at this same table. Pretending to be that kid again, pretending this was nothing more than a sleepover at Tara's grandmother's house, would be so wonderful. I visualized the bedroom at the top of the stairs with two single beds covered with quilts that Nancy had made.

"Now, I'm not going to rush you, but I do expect you to tell me what possessed you to walk all the way from Fredericton. First, I am going to call your house and let them know you are here."

I took a spoonful of the rich brown broth, blew on it, then tasted it, letting the flavour register while at the same time deciding where I would begin telling Nancy this story. I could accept what Nancy was offering without undoing any of what I felt the walk had given me. Taking risks, nature, family fun, friends, grief group.

I had to take my own advice. I'd taken risks and immersed myself in nature. Now Nancy was offering friendship, welcoming me into her home. I trusted her and knew she was someone I could open up to. It felt like meeting her on the last part of my walk was meant to be.

She came back into the kitchen and sat down across the table from me. "I just talked to Lesley. She was very relieved to hear that you were all right. I told her you'd be home sometime tomorrow. We can figure that out later. Tonight, we talk and you get a good night's sleep. I imagine you haven't had the most comfortable sleeps the last two nights."

"I cannot even tell you how glad I am that you were getting on that ferry. It would have been my third night sleeping outside and I wasn't looking forward to it. Not that I would have had any choice. I am really glad I didn't have to, though." I scooped up the last spoonful of stew from the bottom of the bowl. "It's been a whole year since Mike died," I began.

In the next few minutes, as I ate a second helping of stew and my third biscuit, I told Nancy pretty much everything about the last few months. I told her what had happened between Tara and me. I didn't hold back my feelings of anger, especially toward Dad and Jenny. I talked about how alone I had been feeling and how afraid I was for Mom and for our whole family.

"I thought if I went to the concert that they would finally wake up to what was happening."

"I see. You wanted them to miss *you*."

"Yes. I kept telling myself I had to go because it was Mike's favourite band. I convinced myself I was doing it to get closer to him and do something he would have loved to do. And that was partly true. But the bigger truth is I wanted to be gone long enough and far enough away that Mom would finally realize I was missing. Or that she was missing and hadn't taken the least notice of what I was doing in months. I emailed Aunt Lesley just to make sure Mom would realize I was gone, because I wasn't sure she would even know or care. I honestly didn't know what else to do."

"How was the concert?"

I thought about it. "The concert was amazing. I really did take in the music, thinking about Mike the whole time. And I am really glad I went. But what happened afterwards wasn't great, and maybe I should have seen it coming."

I told Nancy about my new friends, even admitting the drinking, drug use, and Bethany's shoplifting habit. "They aren't friends I can trust. Not like Tara. I'm really sorry for how I treated her. I was angry at her because I thought she didn't understand."

"It's a hard thing for friends and family to know exactly what to do when they haven't dealt with death and loss."

"Do you think she will forgive me?"

"I know she will. I daresay she already has. She's missed you terribly."

"I almost got raped the night of the concert. I let my guard down with this guy and I should have known better. I should have realized what his motive was. I knew he couldn't be trusted. I also knew I couldn't depend on my so-called friends."

"Oh, sweetie. That must have been terrifying."

"I got away from the campsite as fast as I could. I left my

backpack, my phone, my bus ticket, and my money behind. I got out to the road and got a drive to Fredericton with a really nice guy named Mike, coincidently, and his mother."

"So that's how you ended up in Fredericton all by yourself. Why didn't you call home?"

"I thought about it, but something kept telling me I had to figure my own way out of the mess I was in. I had made my bed and I had to lie in it, like my grandmother Darrah always used to say. It was the bed I chose that got me in trouble. I took Ethan's offer to sleep in his tent, not even considering that he would take that as an invitation. Mike always told me about him and I should have been smarter."

"You were smart enough to get away when you did. Another good saying is hindsight is 20/20. Do you know what that means?"

"Yeah. I guess so."

"Why don't you go upstairs and have a nice hot shower? I laid out one of my nightgowns and a housecoat. I'm going to put my groceries away and clean up. When you come down we'll talk some more."


I let the hot water beat down on my head and run over my face. It was so easy to talk to Nancy. My grandmother Darrah had died when I was ten, and I never knew my other grandmother. Nancy seemed to understand everything. I wasn't even embarrassed telling her about Ethan. She hadn't blamed me but said I had been smart and did the right thing. I squirted the body wash into my open palm, smelling the fruity smell as I lathered it on my body.

My body. I thought again how thankful I was that I had not been sleeping undressed in that tent. I thought, too, of the instinct I'd had immediately when that truck driver made his creepy remarks. I was in charge of my body and my mind. I possessed inner strength and wisdom and needed to trust myself. I could muster courage when I needed to and I would find a way to make things better. I was almost ready to go home and face that challenge.

I curled up on the couch across from the armchair where Nancy was sitting knitting a long orange blanket.

"I'm making this afghan for Tara's mother. She just got new furniture in their family room and this orange will look lovely on it. You need to go by and visit. They will all love to see you."

"I will. Nancy, I met a girl in Fredericton when Mike and his mom dropped me off. She and her mom are Syrian. They left Syria and walked all the way to a camp in Lebanon. I knew right away she was a friend and she helped remind me what friendship really is. Tara is and has always been that kind of friend."

"Is that what made you think you needed to walk home?"

"Yes. I was so impressed with her story I thought I needed to show that kind of courage. I thought that maybe if I managed to walk all the way home, I could be brave enough to fix my family."

"Is that what you think you need to do, fix your family?"

"Someone has to," I answered.

"I suppose you have heard people say that time heals? People have lots of theories about what a person needs to do to get over a loss. Most of the people with those theories have no idea what they're talking about. Oh, I'm sure there is something to the seven stages of grief and all that, but really, when it comes right down to it, there is nothing that makes actually going through them any easier."

Nancy stood up and walked across the room to a trunk. She reached in and got out another ball of orange yarn. Sitting down, she attached the new ball to the string hanging from her knitting.

"I am going to tell you my story, my loss and experience. I don't claim to have all the answers, but I'm going to tell you what it was like for me. Maybe you'll see your mom in a different way. I think you have a lot to offer, and your own experience has already taught you volumes, but I'm going to tell you loss from a mother's perspective, something you don't have yet and hopefully will never have. Losing a child is a sorrow like no other."

Nancy took a deep breath, as if the task she was setting for herself required all the strength she could muster. "Do you remember the day you and Tara played in the old foundation and I got so angry at you?"

I nodded.

"A house used to stand on that foundation. It was an old house, old when we moved into it. Probably over a hundred years old. Drafty, with uneven floors. My husband's great-grandfather had built it. It burned down."

Again, Nancy paused. "I was in the hospital. Tara's dad was two days old. Probably a flue fire, they said. It was a cold January night and Weldon had likely stocked the furnace full. Weldon was my first husband. The fire started in the night and the old place burned like a tinderbox. Weldon died trying to get our three children out of their beds."

Nancy set her knitting down reaching for a tissue. She wiped the tears dripping down her cheeks. She blew her nose and continued.

"Victoria was nine, George was seven, and Mary Beth was three. I slept the night in the General Hospital with my newborn son in a crib beside me, not knowing that my entire life was burning to the ground."

"Oh, Nancy. That is awful. I'm so sorry. Does Tara know?"

"She knows her dad had two sisters and a brother that died, but I don't think her dad has ever told her how. Even when he was growing up, I didn't talk about them much. I couldn't. I had two more children with my second husband, and they were the siblings Terry knew, and he thought of John as his father.

"I am not saying that not talking about them was the right way. It was just the way we did it. Terry didn't remember them, of course, and I saw no reason to make him grieve for them. Thank goodness he has no memory of those first few years. If he does, it would be my sister Marion he remembers. She cared for him for two years when I was not able. You say this first year has been really hard for your mom. I was two full years before I had any desire to keep living. I was broken, completely stripped of every trace of who I had been before that night. My husband was dead, along with my three beautiful children. I could barely hold my new baby. I could not allow myself to love again, knowing how painful it was when those you loved could be taken so quickly. I had no faith, no hope, no idea how to go from my despair to anything else."

Nancy dabbed her eyes again, then reached for a basket by her feet. She placed the yarn, needles, and knitting on the top, then stood up.

"Franny, I'm going to stop for now. You look exhausted. I'll cook a good breakfast for you when you wake up in the morning. We'll talk some more then and you can decide what you want to do. I can drive you home, but if you want to keep with your plan to walk home, I'll respect that."

I walked across the room and hugged Nancy. This amazing, funny, strong woman had lost a husband and three children. She had been in a place of total despair and somehow come back from it. She had married John, who I remembered as being a big tease. She had had Tara's Aunt Cora and Uncle Blake, and when they came home for visits they acted like a happy family. I never would have imagined that Nancy's life held such deep sorrow.

In the morning, I sat down to the huge breakfast Nancy had prepared for me. The smells woke me, and at first, I wasn't sure where I was as I opened my eyes. I had slept soundly, barely thinking of the last few days or the day ahead. Now, as I pushed my chair up to Nancy's kitchen table and remembered I had to go home today, I was filled with the mixed emotions of dread and excitement.

"I hope you slept well. Have you decided if you want me to drive you home?"

"I thought maybe I'd get you to drive me to Gondola Point and I would walk home from there."

"That sounds like a good plan. I hope I wasn't too hard on you last night. When I say a mother's grief is different from any other, I certainly don't mean to downplay your own grief. You have had to live this last year without the big brother you loved so dearly. You have also had to watch what it has done to your mother, your whole family, and the life you lived before he died. There is nothing easy about any of it. I often feel thankful that Terry didn't have to suffer, being an infant. It still affected him, though. He got a different life, a different father, and a much different mother than he would have had if the fire had never happened."

Nancy walked over to the stove and brought back another pancake, dropping it onto my plate, then sat down and began spreading jam on her toast. "I tried not to suffocate Terry, Cora, and Blake with my worry. A mother who has not lost a child has more confidence in her control. She still believes if she says the right things, like, 'Be careful, wear your bicycle helmet, don't smoke cigarettes, call for a drive,' all the right things to protect her children from all the dangers that can hurt them, she can keep them safe. A mother who has faced the unimaginable reality of a loss no longer has that false hope. She knows that in the blink of an eye, everything she thought could never happen can happen. The horror of that realization is possibly the worst barrier to healing. That and the anger she feels for others who still believe they can prevent things from happening to their children by being the perfect mother. Somehow, other people can make a grieving mother feel the blame for their loss. People don't usually say it aloud, but there's this impression that if you'd just been a better, more careful mother, you wouldn't have lost your child.

"It took a long time for me to let go of the guilt and the fear. I'm sure that is part of your mother's decision to hide away. Franny, you feel left behind, forgotten, but your mother is protecting herself from the fact that she has no control over your well-being. Mike's death proved that terrible truth. I know it seems like she has stopped caring about you, but actually it is the exact opposite of that."

I soaked up the syrup with my last piece of pancake, thinking about what Nancy was saying. "How did you get better?"

"Time. As I said, I barely even held Terry for almost two years. Luckily, Marion stepped in to mother him until I was finally able to. Hopefully those two years did not scar him too much. I was able then to be a mother again, a mother with a new concept of the fragility and privilege of mothering. I was able to find a place to put the fear and the difficult truths. I found somewhere to keep the anger, too. Your mother will find her way as well. You will help her to do that."

Tears were streaming down my cheeks, and Nancy gently patted my back. This wonderful woman was a living, breathing example that someone can live through hell and still find joy. I knew that she would be there for me and could be there for Mom, too. I was overwhelmed with thankfulness that my walk had brought me to her and to this hope.

"Thank you, Nancy. I'm so sorry that happened to you, and I am so glad you told me about it. Hearing about your experience helps me to understand Mom better. I feel ready to go home."

"Well, let's do up these dishes and we can head out."

"I'm going to call Tara when I get home. I hope you don't mind if I come back with her soon. It's not just your cooking I've missed."

On the drive to Gondola Point, Nancy pulled her car into the yard of the Summerville United Church. She got out and started walking toward the graveyard. I followed her. She knelt and brushed the newly cut grass off the base of the granite marker.

*Weldon Arthurs*
*Victoria, George, Mary Beth*
*Always loved, never forgotten*

I reached out and embraced Nancy, letting my grief mix and mingle with hers in this quiet, sacred place.

"Now, you're sure you don't want me to drive you home?" Nancy said as she pulled out onto the road.

"I'm sure. It won't take me too long to walk home from Gondola Point, and I definitely know what I'm up against, unlike a couple of days ago. I am so glad you came along last night. I'm going to tell Mom your story, if you don't mind. Maybe she could come talk to you sometime."

"Of course. I should have reached out to her sooner. But I think us running into each other was meant to be. I was glad to offer you a place to sleep and hopefully a perspective that will help as you start into your second year without Mike. Time will not take the pain away, but it will help you to bear it. You will be okay."

I reached over and kissed Nancy's cheek before grabbing Amira's backpack and hopping out of the car.

# CHAPTER 17

I barely noticed my surroundings as I walked along the Gondola Point Road, up the Vincent Road, and along the Pettingill to our subdivision. It was just before noon and the traffic was slow. I met a few people walking along the sidewalks. Each familiar stretch was comforting as I attempted to downplay the momentous achievement of arriving at my destination. I was going home with an arsenal of hope and optimism. I didn't know what I was going to find, but I did know that I was prepared to face whatever it was.

I could hear the sound of several lawnmowers as I came to my street, but it was the sound and sight of one in particular that I focused on as I got closer to my house. I saw my dad pushing his green Mastercraft on our front lawn. I stopped a moment, letting that register. Dad had his orange Kubota hat backwards on his head and was wearing his ridiculous green jogging pants.

I could see Mom kneeling at one of her side flowerbeds, a wheelbarrow heaped with raked grass and weeds beside her. A huge clump of hostas sat uprooted a short way from where she was kneeling. She was in the thick of spring gardening.

Jordan ran around the corner of the house and spotted me.

"Franny Bear!" he hollered, and Mom spun around to see me. I let the look on her face sink into my soul. What I saw in her expression was a mixture of surprise, relief, joy, and love. It was the very look I had been desperately craving for months. I walked in a daze toward her as she stood up and ran toward me. The mower stopped, and Dad threw his gloves onto the ground and started toward me, too.

Aunt Lesley and Uncle Craig came around from the backyard, and the reunion was a mix of hugging, crying, and everyone talking at the same time. Jenny came out the front door followed by Riley, who looked confused by the commotion.

It was Mom's embrace I held on to the longest, letting her arms encircle me and feeling the deep emotion of her words. "I am so sorry, Franny. So sorry. I was so worried. So worried and afraid. When Alice called and Sue came by, at least I knew you were okay. Then Nancy called to say you'd be home today. You cannot imagine my relief knowing you hadn't run away for good. I wouldn't have blamed you. I have been so selfish. Please forgive me, Franny. Please forgive me."

Aunt Lesley interrupted the reunion. She took Riley's hand and put her free arm around Mom. "Let's all go into the house. It is so good to see you, Franny. I have lunch ready. Grilled cheese in the shape of elephants, which was Jordan's request. I have the tea made, Marilyn. We can all use a break. You won't believe the goings-on since you've been gone, Franny."

Dad picked up my backpack and I walked into the house with Mom on one side and Dad on the other. I felt like I used to when I would walk in the middle of them holding their hands, letting them lift me into the air. I was walking on my own, but having them by my side was definitely making me feel lifted up. I couldn't have asked for a better homecoming.

My happiness at seeing Dad mowing the lawn and Mom working outside was multiplied when I went inside. It wasn't just the incessant chatter of Jordan and Riley that gave the house a feeling so different than when I left. It was obvious that Mom and Aunt Lesley had been cleaning, and when I went upstairs, the magnitude of that cleaning became clear. Mike's bedroom door was open, and I could see several large garbage bags and a couple of cardboard boxes on the floor. I walked in and sat down on his bed, which was now covered with what appeared to be a brand new bedspread, not Mike's tattered *Star Wars* blanket.

The posters were still on the walls, but his bookshelf was empty. The only things on the shelf above his desk were one Little League and two music festival trophies. I looked in the closet, at empty hangers hanging on the rod. I didn't see Mom walk in and sit beside me.

"We haven't thrown anything away yet. You can keep whatever you'd like."

"Can I have a couple of his posters?"

"Of course. You and Jenny can decide which ones you want. You'll want the Don't Feed the Wolf one, I assume. How was the concert?"

"Oh, Mom. It was amazing. Amazing but really hard. I wanted Mike to be with me so badly."

"I know, sweetie. It was a rough weekend for sure, but I'm so proud of you."

"You're not mad?"

"I have no right to be mad. You did what you had to do, and even though I was angry when Lesley arrived and went up one side of me and down the other, I needed it. That is not to say I am impressed that you went to Fredericton with strangers and I didn't have a clue where you were for the last few days, however."

"I'm sorry."

"We can talk about all that later. I know you haven't had much parenting lately, and we're lucky you didn't get up to a lot worse. Aunt Lesley forced me to take a good, hard look at things." She paused. "I say Aunt Lesley, but really Mike had a lot to do with it, too."

"What do you mean?"

Mom got up and walked across the room. She picked one of Mike's stuffed animals out of the box beside the closet door.

"I woke up in the middle of the night on Saturday. I went to bed knowing you weren't home yet but talked myself into believing you were somewhere with Tara, even though I know you and she haven't been hanging out for months. I woke to the sound of Mike's voice. I was half asleep and confused. For a few seconds, I thought he was calling me and I got up and went to his room."

"Once I was fully awake, I realized where I was but couldn't force myself to leave. I lay down on the bed, letting the smell and feel of your brother surround me. I cried out, begging him to help me. He was telling me I had to start living again. I could almost hear him lecturing me, using all the lines I had used on him over the years. I wept and finally fell asleep."

"Amazing that Mike could be two places at once," I said as I wrapped my arms around Mom. "I felt like he was with *me* that night. He kept me safe when I was...well, in a situation that could have been awful. I'll tell you about that later. He was with both of us."

Mom pointed to the Don't Feed the Wolf poster. She touched the lettering. "The moon was shining on that poster when I came in. He was telling me where you were."

I stood and wrapped my arms around Mom as we hugged and cried.

Lesley stood in the doorway waiting, but Riley burst into the room and joined the huddle.

"Would you like to have this moose, Ri?" Mom asked

Riley hugged the stuffed moose to her chest, announcing, "I'm going to show Daddy!" as she ran from the room and down the stairs.

Mom loosened her hug and continued telling me her story.

"I was still sleeping on Mike's bed when loud pounding woke me up. I opened the back door to Lesley, Craig, and the kids. When she got your email, she and Craig booked flights right away. She said you told her you'd stayed away all night several times without me even realizing it, so she decided not to even call before they came. I was so ashamed by that, Franny. So ashamed that when Lesley, Craig, and the kids got here Sunday morning, I hadn't even realized you weren't in your bed."

Lesley took Mom's arm and led her to Mike's bed, sitting down beside her. I sat on the desk chair across the room.

"It's okay, Marilyn. Take a deep breath. Remember what we said. No going back, only moving ahead." Lesley turned to me. "I honestly didn't know what to expect. I wasn't sure she'd let me in, but I was pretty sure she wouldn't slam the door on Craig and the kids. I'm so glad you emailed me, Franny."

"We had a good cry and a long talk. Your Aunt Lesley didn't hold back. You sure sent the right person, Franny."

"You were ready to hear what I had to say."

"Maybe, but I am so glad Franny did what she did." Mom smiled at me. "Aunt Lesley called your dad and told him he and Jenny had to come home. You did all that, Franny. Thank you."

"I didn't know what else to do. I'm just glad it worked." We fell silent for a minute. Then I asked, "Did you know that Nancy Doherty lost her husband and three children in a fire?"

"Oh my heavens, no, I didn't."

"I stayed there last night. She told me about the fire. Terry was just a few days old. She was still in the hospital with him when her house caught fire and killed the rest of her family. She told me what it was like for her and how long it took her to get better afterwards. She said you could talk to her if you wanted to."

"Oh, that poor woman. That must have been terrible. I would like to talk to Nancy if she wouldn't mind. One of the things Lesley and I decided on as part of the plan to move ahead was that I should join a grief group of some kind."

I smiled a little, thinking of my list of insights that I'd chanted on my walk. Which reminded me: "I walked from Fredericton to the Westfield ferry."

"You what?"

"I walked.

"You walked the whole way?"

"Yes. I would have walked the rest of the way, but I saw Nancy when I was getting on the Westfield ferry, and she took me to her house."

"Were you afraid? Where did you sleep? What did you eat? Where did you use the bathroom?"

"Are you two coming down to eat lunch?" Dad called as he jogged up the stairs.

"She walked all the way from Fredericton to the Westfield ferry, Doug! That's about a hundred kilometres, isn't it?"

Dad stood in the doorway with his phone in hand. "Google Maps says 89.6."

"You took a bus up, didn't you? Why did you walk home?" Aunt Lesley asked.

"I lost my backpack, my phone, my money, and my bus ticket. I got a drive into Fredericton and met a girl from Syria." It was sounding farfetched as I was telling it. I wanted to tell Mom and Dad exactly why I walked and what walking that distance had done for me, but right now didn't seem like the right time.

"But you could have come home with Sue when you saw her. Or you could have called," Mom said.

"I wanted to challenge myself. It wasn't that bad, really. Other people have walked farther and under much more difficult conditions." I stood up.

My dad stood completely still. Weeks ago, I would have bristled at his failure to react, but today it seemed the exact opposite of uncaring. "That's our Franny," he said calmly. "Once she gets something in her head, there's no stopping her. You can tell us all about it later. We've got lots to talk about and all the time in the world to do it." He walked over and pulled Mom to her feet. "We're just glad you're home, Franny Bear—that we're all home."

I waited at Tara's bus stop, not knowing how she'd react to me standing there. I hoped I hadn't missed her bus. I wondered if Nancy had called Tara's mother today, telling her about my visit. I saw the bus approaching and watched as Tara stepped out the door. The look on her face made the waiting worthwhile.

Tara dropped her backpack and wrapped both arms around me, crying as if we were long-lost relatives separated by years and countless hardships. It was a reunion fitting of the sappiest movie, and Tara didn't hold back.

"Franny, Franny," she kept saying. Her tears turned to giggles and she took both my hands jumping up and down. "It is so good to see you. Marin Donavan said at school today that you were missing. She told all around school that you vanished from the campsite. I knew she was being dramatic, because I was sure if you were really missing it would be on the news. And I saw Jenny yesterday. She wasn't acting like you were missing." She picked up her backpack and started walking. "Mom will be so glad to see you."

"I'm sorry I was such a bitch."

"Are you kidding me? It was all my fault. I should have been a better friend. I have missed you so much."

"I went to the Don't Feed the Wolf concert on the weekend. I did vanish from the campsite. Ethan Rogers almost raped me.

"Oh my God. What a creep."

"That's for sure. Remember what Mike used to say about him? He was dead on." I winced at my choice of words. "Tara. I shouldn't have gotten mad at you. You were right. I'm not the only one with problems. Everyone has their own problems. I couldn't see that."

"I feel so awful that I haven't been there for you in the last few months. I never should have said what I said."

"Can we just forget it? It wasn't your fault. I definitely over-reacted. Let's put it behind us. Aunt Lesley and Uncle Craig are here with Jordan and Riley, and Dad and Jenny are home.

They were away most of the winter. Mom has been really depressed and not doing well at all. I'm hopeful, though, that if we all work together, we can help her get to a better place. She's already so much better than when I left for the concert."

"How was the concert, besides the Ethan thing?"

"It was amazing. I kept wishing you were with me. I have missed you so much."

We walked into Tara's backyard and up to her back door. I could not believe how anxious I was to be a part of her family's life again. I would look at Terry differently now, knowing what he had lost, though I didn't expect I would blurt out something stupid about it. I was just happy to have them back as a part of my support system. After my long walk home alone, I knew the neighbours and the friends I could count on.

On my way to Tara's bus stop I had stopped to talk to Mrs. McEachern, who was out walking her dog.

"I'm sorry I lied to you, Mrs. McEachern. I wasn't at a friend's the day you saw me in Oromocto. I was walking home. I walked all the way to the Westfield ferry. I thought if I told you the truth you would make me come home with you."

"Wow, Franny. How long did it take you to walk? Where did you sleep? Why did you do that? You know I would have driven you home."

"I know. But I needed to make myself do it. I really wanted to walk and figure out how I could make things better for my family."

"That was very brave of you. We should have done more to help your mom and your family. I let myself believe that minding my own business was the kindest thing I could do. I was wrong. Friends and neighbours have to stick together."

"It's hard for people to know what the best way to help is. I think Mom knows her neighbours are there for her. Keep coming by. She's getting better."

Mrs. McEachern had hugged me and I hugged her back. For a moment, it felt like it had in the funeral parlour, but I knew her caring was genuine and she was someone I could be honest with.

"I am done with lying and pretending," I'd continued. "I am going to be completely open with people from now on. I will let you know when there's something I think you could do to help. Hiding out and acting like everything is fine doesn't work."

Mom had suggested I wait and go back to school on Monday, but I wanted to face going back before I thought of more reasons to chicken out. At least Ethan wouldn't be there but I wasn't looking forward to seeing Bethany, Marin, and Sam. For one thing, I wasn't anxious to hear their take on why I'd left the campsite. I didn't want to hear any of the crap they had to say and I planned on making it perfectly clear that I was no longer interested in hanging out with them. I wanted my phone and my money, although I figured Bethany would deny there had been any cash in my backpack if she had even bothered to bring it back for me. I was also going to confront her about Mike's ornament.

I stood at my locker, waiting for Bethany to show up. Tara was waiting at the end of the hall, prepared to back me up if Bethany gave me a hard time. I wasn't afraid of Bethany, but I was glad to have Tara nearby. I would make it perfectly clear to Bethany that I was back with my former friends. I had some other things to fix at school as well. Last night I had told Mom and Dad about my failing grades and the possibility I might fail several of my classes.

"It's not your fault," Mom had said. "Maybe if we meet with your teachers and explain things, they can offer you a way to bring up your marks."

"We let you down," Dad added. "I wanted so badly to believe that everything was fine here that I didn't even ask you about school. Jenny and I both realized that when Lesley called. We were running away. Jenny wants to wait until next year to resume her training. She agreed we had to come home and make sure you and Mom were all right."

"We are going to start some family counselling and some individual counselling," Mom continued. "The woman I spoke to yesterday said there are some really good grief counselling services through a group called Gentle Path. We can figure that all out and do what feels right. The most important part right now is being a family again and not keeping everything to ourselves. We have let this last year distance us instead of bringing us closer together. Mike would be so disappointed in us all."

"We'll figure it out, hon," Dad had said, holding Mom while she cried. "It won't do any good beating ourselves up. Our girl pushed us into taking a good hard look at everything and we will find our way. Mike would be proud of you, Franny Bear."

We were all crying by that time, and I even let Jenny hug me before we finally pulled ourselves together. As hard as it was to see them cry and to let myself cry in front of them, it was so much better than the silence and separation we had all gotten so good at.

"The kids and I are staying for June and July," Aunt Lesley stated, coming in at the tail end of our sob fest. "Craig is going back home on Sunday, but he's coming back down for two weeks at the end of July. We rented the cottage from Ernie Gorham. How does everybody feel about a vacation on the peninsula?"

"I think that would be wonderful," Mom said.

"It is so great of you to stay, Lesley," Dad said. "This means the world to your sister, and having those kids around sure helps, too. I was thinking we might come up to Ontario in August to visit you guys. Thought we might all get a day in at Canada's Wonderland."

I had stood staring at my family. Family fun had been on the list of the wisdom my walk gave me. Family fun, grief groups, nature—and here they were, talking about counselling, renting the cottage again, and going to Wonderland. It was exactly what I had hoped for. What was the first one? I tried to remember the rhythmic sound of the list I had recited. I could picture exactly where I had been walking when I turned the list into a song. *Taking risks* and *friends*. It was then I had decided for sure that I would go to school the next day. I knew Tara would be right by my side, and any risk I faced she would face with me.

"Where the hell have you been?" Bethany said as she came up to me. "Thought there'd be a big stink when you didn't get home. Kept waiting for the cops to show up. Where did you take off to? I've got your stuff."

"Do you have my brother's ornament?"

"Yeah, calm down."

"I am calm."

"What, have you got a bodyguard or something?" Bethany sneered, looking toward Tara, who had moved closer. "You still haven't told me where you went. Nobody knew where you'd gone in the morning and then your backpack was still there. Did you meet some hot guy at the concert? You could have told somebody."

"The ornament, please."

"Here." Bethany passed me the Lego ornament, then reached in her locker, pulling out my backpack. "Your cell phone and money's still in there. I sold your bus ticket when you didn't show up. That money's in there, too. How'd you get home, anyway?"

"I walked."

"Yeah, right."

I took my cell phone and money out of the backpack before hanging it on the hook and shutting my locker, starting to walk away, not bothering to give Bethany any more details. She would not understand at all if I tried to tell her why I walked. She obviously didn't know anything about what had happened to make me leave the campsite, and as far as I was concerned it could stay that way.

# CHAPTER 18

Ms. Fullerton assigned me two essays and a reading list to catch me up. Mrs. White scheduled some makeup tests and arranged some after-school tutoring to prepare me for the exam. I was passing Chemistry, which surprised me. It would be a busy, challenging couple of weeks before exams, but at least it now seemed possible I could pass and get all my credits. I even went to Mrs. Taylor and asked her if I could redo my Family Dynamics assignment. I felt I now knew exactly how to design a perfect home. It wouldn't make a difference in my mark, but I wanted to do it anyway. It somehow felt like a way to undo the misery of the months since I'd let Bethany do the assignment for me.

Mom and I drove to Fredericton one weekend to see Amira and Miriam. Amira and I watched as our mothers embraced and cried in each other's arms, barely able to speak the same language but fully understanding the language of pain and loss. We went together to the Diplomat and enjoyed the buffet, even though Miriam argued she could cook us a meal instead of wasting money at a restaurant. Mom told her it was the least she could do after the hospitality Amira had shown me.

Afterwards we returned to their small apartment, and it was there I started thinking about the assignment I wanted to redo. A perfect home had absolutely nothing to do with size, furnishings, or any of the things Bethany had written about when she did the assignment for me. I knew it sounded corny and cliché to say a perfect home had to do with love, but it was profoundly clear as I looked at Amira and Miriam welcoming us into their home and offering us what little they had. What made a perfect home was exactly that: love.

Since I'd returned from my walk, the Callaghan home was a clear contrast to the empty home it had been, despite the number of rooms, the number of televisions, fibre optic TV and Internet, running water, and all the rest of the luxuries we took for granted. Now there were laughter, conversation, hugs, tears, meals together, and all the other things I had missed so desperately.

The sadness still lingered. Of course it did. It was still so hard to sit across the table from the spot Mike always sat, even though Riley or Jordan usually fought to sit there. Jenny and I had gone through the boxes and bags, deciding on the things we couldn't part with. I drank from Mike's *Give a hoot—Play the flute* mug every morning. His Don't Feed the Wolf poster hung over my bed, and Jenny had hung the vintage Woodstock poster over hers. Riley barely put down the stuffed moose and usually fell asleep with her arms wrapped around it.

A week later, the whole family met with a woman named Valerie, a family counsellor. She met with us as a group first, then individually with each of us. She gave us homework. Mine was to look at the decisions I had made in the last year and decide if I could fix some of the consequences. A do-over, she called it, and part of what I decided I needed to do included this assignment.

The other, more challenging, task was calling Bethany and meeting with her to talk about some things. I didn't know why it seemed so important, and, believe me, I tried to talk myself out of it. I was quite willing to pretend the months I had hung out with her hadn't even happened, but for some reason, every time I looked at Mike's Lego ornament, now displayed on my dresser, I felt the need to reach out to Bethany, and so I texted her.

She called me right away. She sounded genuinely pleased to hear from me and asked me to come to her place. On the walk over, I couldn't even imagine how the meeting was going to go. Mom wanted to drive me and wait for me, but I convinced her I would be fine to walk and told her I'd call her to come get me when I was ready to come home.

"I thought you were done with me," Bethany said when she opened the door.

"Is your mother home?" I asked.

"No, she has a new boyfriend, and she's there most of the time. I don't care that much, as long as she keeps paying the rent."

I walked in and kicked off my sandals, although from the look of the place, wearing my footwear wouldn't make the apartment any dirtier. I moved some stuff off the couch and sat down. "I wanted to come by and talk about a couple of things. As you already know, I'm hanging out with my friend Tara and my old group of friends again."

"Yeah. It didn't take a rocket scientist to figure that out. Even Marin and Sam aren't having much to do with me these days. Things kind of went south after the long weekend. For one thing, it pissed me off that they weren't more sympathetic after the whole Ethan Rogers thing."

"What Ethan Rogers thing?" My heart was pounding. Maybe they did know what happened to me and why I left the campsite.

"Well, I was stupid enough to think I was dating the guy, and they told him when I thought I was pregnant. Believe me, when he got wind of that he was long gone. Apparently two bastard kids is his quota. Thank God I started my period."

"When did you start dating Ethan?"

"Great question. I guess having sex and waking with him

naked beside me was our first date. He was all gushy for a couple of weeks. I guess I was good enough to warrant coming back for more."

"Was the first time at the campground?"

"Yeah."

I felt sick to my stomach. Ethan Rogers hadn't bothered coming after me. He probably hadn't even skipped a beat before crawling out of his tent and into Bethany's. I wondered how long it took him to realize I wasn't coming back before he decided on his next option. Apparently, it didn't matter one bit who he got it from—just as long as he got it.

"Ethan tried to rape me that night," I said. "That's why I left the campsite and wasn't there in the morning. Did he rape you?"

"I was drunk earlier, but I knew what was going on when he crawled in my tent and woke me up. I'm not proud of it, but I did participate."

"Bethany. Ethan Rogers is a disgusting pig. He knew you'd been drinking. He'd told me earlier that you'd passed out. You can say you participated, but he was taking advantage of the fact you were sound asleep and probably still drunk. Not fighting him off is not the same as giving consent. He had no right to take advantage of your state."

"I figured out what had happened when you weren't there in the morning, but at first I didn't want to believe it. For a couple of days I thought he really liked me. Just one more thing for me to be ashamed about. You had the self-confidence and pride to say no to the bastard. I just let him use me like I let everybody else use me. God forbid Bethany Thompson should stand up for herself."

I looked over and saw tears streaming down Bethany's cheeks. I was completely shocked at the depth of emotion I was witnessing. "It wasn't your fault. What he did is not okay. And for me it was luck more than confidence or pride. Ethan Rogers is the one who should feel ashamed."

"I'm sorry, Franny," Bethany said.

"Sorry for what?" I asked.

"For a whole lot of things, but mostly for stealing your brother's ornament."

I didn't answer.

"I know I never lost a brother like you did. I technically never even had a brother, but there was this one kid. Justin. Mom and I lived with his dad for three years and I really liked that kid. I loved him, I guess, for all the good that did. He was two years younger than me and he loved Lego. He built amazing stuff. His dad took him and all his Lego and I never saw the kid again. It hit me that night at your house when I took the ornament out of the box just how much I missed him."

It was my turn to apologize, and I *was* sorry, for what I saw as a deep sorrow Bethany usually stuffed down. "Do you know where Justin lives? Maybe someday you can see him."

"What good would that do? He wasn't really my brother. He probably couldn't care less. I know his father couldn't." She got up and walked over to the kitchen table, reaching for a cigarette. "Want one?"

"No. I don't smoke, remember? I don't do half the stuff I let on I did when I hung out with you guys. You might think I'm a loser, but I don't apologize for who I am. I guess I wanted to come by and clear that up. I don't want to be a bitch about it, but I am not into the same stuff as you are."

Bethany laughed without sounding at all happy. "Franny, *I'm* not even into this stuff. God. Sometimes I look around and wonder what the hell I've gotten myself into. I wouldn't mind trying to be a bit more like you instead of the other way around. I guess the Ethan thing was kind of a wake-up call. I don't want to be my mother. But it seems like I'm going to have to make more of an effort to not turn out that way. For starters, I need to graduate and possibly even go to university." She looked embarrassed for a second. "I know it's going to sound stupid, but I've actually always wanted to be a teacher. I just don't know if it's possible, you know?" She gestured at the grim apartment.

"Why don't you start hanging out with Tara and me? We can show you the fine art of being boring losers."

We talked about a lot of other things before I called Mom to come get me. I asked her if Bethany could come for supper and was so pleased when she said yes. Jordan and Riley took to Bethany as if they had always known her. She taught Jordan to tie his shoes when he wouldn't even try before. She did seem to have a way with kids.

I had already turned off my light and was playing my Don't Feed the Wolf album, the volume low, hoping it would lull me to sleep, when Jenny knocked on my door.

"Can I talk to you?" Jenny said.

"Sure, come on in." I turned on my lamp and reached for the remote to mute the music.

"You can leave the music on," Jenny said. She sat down on the edge of my bed. "They're playing in Brampton in August, you know. Maybe we can talk Mom and Dad into letting us go see them while we're at Aunt Lesley's."

"Yeah. That would be great."

"I need to talk to you, Franny. I have not been a very good sister."

Jenny started to cry and I reached for a tissue to give her. I really didn't know what to say. Thinking back to the months when all my thoughts toward her had been filled with resentment and anger, I didn't feel like I was ready to tell her she was a great sister. I waited for her to continue.

"Valerie told me to write down my thoughts and straighten out some stuff. Basically, she told me I had to look at the motivation behind my obsession with competing these last few months."

Jenny took a piece of paper out of her housecoat pocket, unfolding it, her hands shaking a bit. "I do love to skate, and

I thought that was my main motivation. I've always been competitive, but I don't need to tell you that."

"No, you don't. Having a little sister better than me at just about everything makes that pretty clear."

"Well, I'll tell you something you've been way better at than me, and that's dealing with losing Mike. You've been so brave and so honest about it and I've been running away from it. Skating away from it, maybe. I've been really selfish, too, and I'm so sorry for that. When I let myself write whatever came to my head instead of just writing the expected reasons, I kept coming back to the same reason: I wanted Dad's attention. I wanted to matter. I wanted to be the one he focused on. What kind of a selfish monster am I that thought I needed to drag Dad away from home and have him all to myself?"

I reached out and put my arm around Jenny. "You're not a monster, Jenny. I've thought all those same things. I've been so angry that no one was paying any attention to me. I have even been angry at Mike sometimes for dying and ruining everything. We're just kids. We don't know how to handle all this. Mom and Dad don't even know. We have to find our way, and at least we're starting to try. Mom was in really bad shape. I left on the long weekend hoping to force her to see that, and I wrote to Aunt Lesley for her help." I paused. "And, if I'm being completely honest, I also left to get Mom and Dad's attention."

"Can you ever forgive me for getting so wrapped up in myself that I left you to deal with her, with everything, by yourself?"

"Of course. I was so happy to see you walk out the front door when I got home. Every bit of anger evaporated when I saw the look on your face when you saw me. These last couple of weeks have been so good. I am so glad you are home and staying home, but I don't want you to have to give up your dreams. Mike would not want us to stop doing the things we love."

"I do love skating, but I'm not as good as Dad has convinced himself. I'm not going to give it up, but I'm putting my family first. I won't even think about training again till fall. I'm going to be honest with myself for a change, and I'm going to spend time with my big sister."

I stared at the computer screen, the words blurry through my tear-filled eyes. My essay might seem corny and sappy, but I believed wholeheartedly in the words I had written. I didn't care if anyone else understood them. I didn't even really care if Mrs. Taylor took the time to read them, and I didn't expect her to change my mark. I wrote them because I lived them and I knew them to be true. Lately, I could see the lessons I had learned over the last few months and the terrible reality of losing my big brother as a possible answer to my question about what my talent was. Maybe I could help more people than just my own family to see the things that matter. Maybe the wisdom I found on my long walk home was something I could share with others. Maybe Franny Callaghan had something to offer after all.

### A Perfect Home

*A home is a shell, four walls that hold a family. A family is made of people bound together by love. Families sometimes change and grow, and sometimes loss and sorrow shape and mold a family into something different from what it was. In the midst of change and challenge, the same things matter—and none of those things can be bought at Costco.*

*Families support each other. They let each other cry and hold each other until the crying stops. A family laughs and plays and works together. A family forgives and asks for forgiveness. A family makes mistakes and learns from life's hard lessons. A family talks to one another and listens and hears and waits for the words that matter. A family remembers and celebrates. A family believes in the power and strength of each individual member and is rebuilt when it suffers great loss.*

*A perfect home is not built or bought or designed. It cannot be found in the real estate listings. It doesn't matter what country, what city, what community it's in. A perfect home is wherever the family finds itself and can withstand the struggles and difficulties real life throws its way. A perfect home and a perfect family look far from perfect. Courage and determination lie beneath and hold the home and family together.*

*Creating a perfect home is like chiselling stone or shaping clay. It is molded and fired in a blazing kiln. It is anchored and fixed with the weight of love and loyalty. It is built without blueprints and within its flaws lies its deepest beauty. To describe such perfection is as futile as counting grains of sand or keeping an inventory of the stars in the sky.*

Mrs. Taylor, I laid it on a little thick, especially in that last paragraph, and I don't expect a better mark...but at least I wrote it myself this time.

Franny Callaghan

# Acknowledgements

Thank you to Terrilee Bulger and Acorn Press. Thanks again to Penelope Jackson for her editing guidance, patience, and insight. Thanks to Matt Reid for the cover design.

I needed some generational guidance for this one, and Crystal and Mya offered me that. It appears I'm getting old. I also take something away from each school I visit, and I thank all the students who welcome me so warmly. Tori and Hadyn come to mind among the many kids I've had the pleasure to meet in the last while. They keep me somewhat in the know.

Thanks to my people who carry me along in every way that matters: Burton, Meg, Cody, Emma, Paige, Chapin, Brianne, Anthony, Skyler, Bella, Caleb, and Ashlie. And to the memory of our beloved Zac.